Wedding in October

Wedding in October

a novel

Geoffrey Clark

Red Hen Press Los Angeles 2002

WEDDING IN OCTOBER

Cover image "Past Dreams" by David Winston
Book and cover design by Mark E. Cull

ISBN 1-888996-36-6
Library of Congress Control Number 2001090071
Published by Red Hen Press

First Edition

Printed In Canada

In memory of
Elmer Clayton "Dick" Hunt
1870-1950
and his wife
Agnes "Auntie" Hunt
1880-1967

Table of Contents

These sweeps of light undo me.
Look, look, the ditch is running white!
I've more veins than a tree!
Kiss me, ashes, I'm falling through a dark swirl.

—Roethke, "The Lost Son"

Chapter One

There was going to be a wedding at the Champs!

I'm nineteen and a senior at the Ermine Falls School—Turner Springstead, my father, kept me back from school until I was seven—and my friend Doc Knowles, who's twenty and already a sophomore at Central State in Mt. Haven where he's studying to be a veterinarian, recently explained how the Champs got its name: 'Over the years everybody kind of shortened it until it lost the Frenchy part and now it's 'The Champs,'—but it's really *Les Champs du Roi*, *Lay Shawn Doo-Wah*, translates to 'the fields of the king,' or so Renfrew says . . ."

Doc's real name is Clayton, and he's the one guy outside of my family I'd go to for advice on anything: he's sane and funny, loose-limbed and affable, red-haired and freckled like his old man, Odell. Like my brother Rex, he's the guy you want on your side if you're in a fix. He's got the kind of reliability that's bred in the bone—which is what I'd like people to say of me.

"Where'd it originally come from?"

"Well, the LaBaughs are French all right, but I dunno—seems likely that 'bout five acre field there on your right when you come around the circle drive is the 'Shawns' part of it, or so Renfrew once told me, Miller . . . of course it also could be he's full of shit . . ."

"Guess it doesn't much matter anyhow . . ."

"Nah—that it's there's what counts, you and Rex'll have a hell of a time, wish I could be there . . ."

Doc's been kitchen boy at the Champs the last couple of summers, and the manager, Sheldon Renfrew, promised him he'd be Assistant Cook next season, the summer of '59.

Rex is my elder by two years, and we've done odd jobs out at the American Plan resort, just six miles northeast of our hometown Ermine Falls for years. In fact, it was there that just this past summer Rex fell hook, line and sinker for an empty-headed but nonetheless cute waitress named Raina Frucht (as in *Frooked*) and she dumped him—his hangdog look was for real and lasted for quite a while. Maybe it's still there hiding somewhere behind his eyes.

Before, it'd never occurred to me a guy like my brother would fall into what he was always cautioning me against with a woman, and so walk right into what he was used to dishing out.

Some might say, "Serves 'im right." Not me. Nor Turner (if he knew, and perhaps he did); it may be just three of us batching it, but we're a family and a whole hell of a lot tighter than most.

* * *

My talk with Doc was a little over a month ago, just before he left for CSU and I started my last year at the Ermine Falls School. And now it was Friday, the tenth of October, 1958, and by God there was going to be a wedding at the Champs.

The college kids who staffed the place during the summer had all gone back to their schools, mostly Michigan State and the U of M, so here was an opportunity for Rex and me to have some fun and pick up a little change—we were so trusted by the LaBaughs we usually worked without supervision and kept track of our own hours.

Later, after the present doings were over, we'd make some more for muscling up the heavy shutters for the sixteen cottages, the lodge and kitchen-dining-room complex and generally putting the spread away for winter.

Rex was pretty handy at cooking so he'd be helping the pastry cook, Ardis Gray from nearby Deer Rapids, do such cooking as was to be done—certainly it'd be nothing as elaborate as when the place was, as they said, "in season."

Me, I'd do whatever they told me to. Happily.

The owners, the LaBaughs (Lah-Baw), would mostly all be there with friends, many of them regular summer people, and probably some hangers-on and relatives we'd never seen: surely some novelties would come our way.

The focal point would of course be the petite and strikingly pretty blond LaBaugh princess, twenty-six-year-old Clover, who tomorrow would marry Jefferson Davis Budlong, an "up-and-coming" attorney from Richmond who resembled G. Mennen "Soapy" Williams, Michigan's governor, except that Jeff Budlong's chestnut hair was short, in contrast to our governor's long combed-straight-back gray-shot black hair.

The LaBaughs had owned the resort since it'd been built around the turn of the century, and clearly it was a family enterprise designed for fun and not a money-maker, a place for the family to spend their summers "resorting," as they said around these parts. That was understood by my own neighbors to be a generally frantic pursuit of tennis, boating, fishing, waterskiing, sailing, and any other unproductive pastimes the lake, grounds and local territory were good for.

To make the LaBaugh's concentration on fun worry-free, Sheldon Renfrew relieved the family of all but executive decisions and of all else that was commonly regarded as work. Renfrew taught high school civics in Traverse City and his management services each summer no doubt nicely enhanced his income. He'd been the Champs' official manager for years.

The LaBaughs, from what I could see, had things just the way they wanted them: Water sports. Tennis, tennis, tennis. And golf and sailing and bridge parties, all accompanied by considerable but seldom excessive drinking. If other intrigues were afoot, I knew little of them, save what I could surmise from glimpses and guesses, likely feeble indices of what was really going on.

* * *

On this Friday afternoon before the Saturday wedding, Rex and I were at home getting our stuff together up in the attic we shared. Downstairs Turner sat at the dining room table, listening to the news from NBC in New York City on his Hallicrafter's Sky Buddy and reading a three-day-old *New York Times* he'd found in a car he'd bought at auction. At least once a month he and Rex went to Lansing with our flatbed truck to pick up likely late-model wrecks which were our biggest moneymakers in the yard, along with Turner's specialty, rebuilt truck transmissions. A totalled car bought for $200 might eventually yield several times that much from selling the parts off one at a time, if you had the patience. Patience was a quality Turner used to lack, according to him, though Rex and I hadn't been old enough to see much of whatever his former self had demonstrated. Anyhow, he seemed to have somehow discovered and brought patience back with him from the South Pacific.

* * *

I watched Rex put spare jeans, socks, his swimming trunks, a big beach towel, his shaving kit and some other odds and ends in the athletic satchel he ordinarily used for his baseball stuff. He tossed a box of a dozen lubricated Ramses ("Lubricated is always good, Miller, if you think y' might have to speed things along, y' know?") on top of the stuff, then zipped the bag up.

"Jesus," I said, "you're an optimistic son of a bitch—a dozen rubbers? You don't really think there's gonna be *that* much likely quiff around? If you were to use 'em all up that'd mean you'd be getting laid four times a day for each of three days, if you spaced it out even . . ."

"Well, you just never know . . . 'Be Prepared,' like the Boy Scouts say, huh? Here, you might's well be prepared too . . ." He tossed a box of three White Trojans onto my bunk.

That hadn't occurred to me, and I was so struck by the notion that I could feel a little buzzing in my balls and the beginnings of a boner.

I didn't say anything else but continued to pack my army surplus knapsack: underwear, a spare pair of jeans, jean cut-offs, swimming trunks (taking my cue from Rex—it was still warm enough to swim in Lake Albion, at least if, according to Rex, you had a little hair on your ass), my black hooded sweatshirt, sweat socks, shaving kit, toothbrush, and two rolls of Life Savers. I was sure there'd be plenty of soap, towels and washcloths in the Champs' laundry. I stuffed the Trojans into a sweat sock and stuck it down the sleeve of my sweatshirt. Then I tossed in two paperbacks, *Renaissance Poetry, Volume III*, edited by Leonard Dean, and *The Viking Portable Chekhov*, the latter lent to me by Doc, and cinched the pack's straps. There would no doubt be some slack moments when I could read.

We quickly policed up our quarters and went downstairs.

Rex was lithe, dark and handsome, like Tom Mix in the comic books, and there was eagerness in his springy step and in the jaunty way he held his satchel as he descended quickly before me down the steep narrow staircase, me steadying myself by my hand on the brick chimney. It was cool to the touch now, and I thought about how in the winter the bricks radiated enough heat to almost keep us warm—which in turn made me think of how, after the sun had set at the Champs during the summer, you could walk along the cement pathways and feel its warmth on your bare soles.

I stopped for a moment and sniffed Hoppe's Nitro Solvent #9 in the air—Rex cleaned his guns once a month whether they needed it or not. For some reason the solvent's familiar tang almost brought tears to my eyes. Each time I left home overnight some part of me always feared something would happen and I'd never be able to get back.

* * *

Turner, seated at the dining room table, looked up from the *Traverse City Record Eagle*. A newscaster on Turner's Hallicrafter's Sky Buddy was telling us that President Eisenhower had ordered federal agencies to cut their employment levels 2 percent for fiscal 1959 to make up for a pay raise voted by Congress.

Turner regarded us, his upper lip losing that curl of contempt the news, to which he was more or less addicted, sometimes produced.

Turner liked plenty of sugar and milk in his coffee and didn't mind at all when it got tepid or even cool.

Just now he had half a cup of just-drawn steaming coffee in his cup and was about to fill it to its top from a waxed half-pint container of milk—our milk cow, Elizabeth, had died two years earlier and we'd taken to buying milk at the store.

The container, the same kind we'd gotten at school lunches for years, looked small in Turner's large hand, and for some reason it was satisfaction bordering on delight to watch as with great deliberation Turner tilted the waxed carton and let the milk run in a thin trickle into the cup until it was nearly full.

Little Bohemia

August, 1945

It's a Wednesday in August.

I have never been in such a place as Little Bohemia in Traverse City before. It's dark, smoky, with a smell that makes your nose wrinkle up, sort of like down in Sonney's root cellar, where he keeps potatoes and carrots and turnips in a square hole in the dirt he keeps covered with canvas and a square of plywood. And there're jars of preserves and canned goods, mainly whole tomatoes, pickles, corn relish and grape jelly on shelves along the wall. A cask of Sonney's homemade grape wine lies down on a little sawhorse he made for it.

One smell I recognize for sure is beer. Often when Sonney comes in from a day's haying in summer, Pearl will open a bottle of Stroh's and pour him a glass and put it in front of him on the oilcloth-covered kitchen table. He'll drink it slowly, the way Rex and I eat ice cream cones. Sonney'll sit there for about five minutes after he's drunk the glass, then he'll get up and slowly go to the icebox for the bottle with the remaining third in it. He'll pour it all at once into his glass. The foam will climb up the glass and Sonney will watch intently as it slowly melts. Then all at once he'll drink it down in two gulps and go in and sit in his big chair beside his Atwater-Kent console with the green tuning eye and listen to Gabriel Heatter give the war news. The more it sounds like we're beating the Japs, the more excited Sonney gets.

Seated now at this small round table for four in Little Bohemia, Sonney says, "When the Japs are finished, Miller, that's when you guyses' Pa'll come home—don't you worry, you and Turner and Rex are all gonna be together again . . ." (I don't worry, haven't worried. I can't really remember what Turner looks like; I like living with Pearl and Sonney and Rex just fine, can't see any need for any changes even if my father comes home.)

"Know what General Buckner said 'fore the Jap sonsabitches killed him with a lucky shell, Miller? He said you just gotta march into their country and make 'em realize their complete goddamn defeat!"

Sonney seems to realize he's let his voice get a little loud so he lowers it: "Well, no, he didn't say 'goddamn' but the rest he did . . . Buckner, there was a man. Tough. Strong. Could march with a full pack and outdo his troops. He ran the Tenth Army, Miller, while it's the Fourth Marines your daddy is in . . ."

Over in the corner farthest from us a song begins on the jukebox, one that usually causes Sonney to change the station when it comes on the little radio he keeps in his blacksmith shop:

"Oh, mairzy doats and doazy doats
And little lambsy-divey
Kiddley-divey too, wouldn't you . . ."

Sometimes at home, as Sonney watches the foam in his glass from that last third of the bottle go down, I'll crawl up on his lap and take out what he calls his railroad watch on its leather strap and press it to my ear and listen to it tick and he'll offer me a sip. I always take the glass he puts into my hands and bring it to my lips, then I smell and wrinkle my lips and shove it back at him to say, "How could anybody like this stuff?"

There's a glass of beer in front of him now on this little round table in Little Bohemia, what Pearl calls a "beer garden" and what Sonney calls a "gin mill." They're always making jokes about this place and about beer gardens and gin mills in general.

It's a big glass and it was brought to Sonney full to the brim with just a light froth by a tired-looking woman—I wonder if back over there by the bar, where there are stools and a brass rail and a mirror and a guy behind the bar and a cash register, if there's a huge beer bottle that still has a third left in it.

So far Sonney's only taken a sip. He keeps looking around for somebody. Then his big rough chapped hands clutch at the edge of our table and he's looking hard over where the door's swung open and somebody's there but you can't quite see who because the light's too bright.

Sonney relaxes, sits back in the creaking round-bottom

wooden chair, and in a moment John Presley from town is sitting down with us, giving me a smiling nod and a "How-do." John's Sonney's age, sixty-something, and lives in a little log cabin not far from the Ermine Falls School. Sometimes kids who take a path past his place when they walk from school to town try to peep through the windows and holler, "Hey Johnny! Crazy Johnny!" Back before John got arthritis in his hands and rheumatiz in his back, Sonney said they worked together on most of the barn raisings in Skeegemog County. And he said John used to be able to pick huckleberries faster than anyone he ever saw.

* * *

"It's been a while, eh, John?" John's what Sonney calls himself, "an old-timer." Old timers like to sit around and talk about the "olden days" when things were better. Like Sonney, John's lean and leathery, with bright dark eyes and deep creases in his cheeks.

"We definitely ain't got too many more days of sitting around gin mills sipping drafts left," John says. "We might's well make use of every chance we get . . ."

"Yeah," Sonney says, "Christ, these days I feel like just another old fool out in my old Model A truck kind of humping along the road about thirty or so and, Christamighty, all them bloods in their V-8's nipping around me like I'm standing still . . . almost hate to come out and put a fine young feller like this one here into harm's way."

He reaches across the table as if to cuff my head but doesn't.

"Well, let's hope you're right. The goddamned Japs are about all washed up . . . hope when we overrun'em they get a bunch of tanks and dozers and run all the little yellow sonsabitches into the Pacific Ocean . . ."

"Well, how's about the kids?" I ask. Sonney is always telling me to "get an oar in."

John sits back in his chair like I shot him, like he just saw me, like I'd been sort of like that big parcel wrapped up and sitting on the fourth chair at our table that Sonney got at Monkey Ward's when we were walking here from the municipal parking lot. John considers what I asked for several seconds, then says slowly, "No, no, I ain't for doing nothing like that to women nor children nor old folks, Miller, just the military, them big-teethed yellow sonsabitches that bombed Pearl Harbor and killed our brothers and fathers and sons willy-nilly at Iwo Jima and Corregidor and Bataan and the Solomons. And 'specially them bunch of a-tawls comes under the name of Tarawa where your daddy fought them dirty little bastards, pardon my French. Maybe we'll bring somea' them women and kids back over here to God's Country so they can learn to not be so goddamn bloodthirsty."

The tired-looking woman sets a glass of beer like Sonney's in front of John and conversation stops.

Sonney seems a little surprised I spoke up like I did, and he says to John Presley, "I been telling Miller he's got to learn to stick up for himself, to get his oar in and to learn how things work so's he don't get flim-flammed. Turner'll show him and Rex how to handle things when he gets back . . ."

John says something softly to Sonney but I hear: "Yeah, long's Turner ain't got his love affair with John Barleycorn goin' on things'll be jake . . ."

Sonney turns and looks John in the face. He's a little angry, because his voice lowers and he speaks more slowly than usual. "Each V-Mail I get, Johnny, he writes 'No drinking' under his name. I figure he's gonna make it back and be together with his fellers again—soon's the goddamned Japs fold up like a pup tent . . ."

There's about a third left in Sonney's glass, so I reach out and my fingers circle the big glass's cold middle where it squeezes in like Pearl's egg timer. I pull the glass part-way towards me. "How's about I have my sip now?"

Sonney smiles, and so does John Presley.

"Go 'head," he says.

I pull the heavy glass close and bring it slowly up to my lips. I always wrinkle my nose and sometimes make a sound like "Ugh" before I push it away, shaking my head. Pearl usually smiles even though she says she doesn't think it's very funny.

This time I grip the glass with both hands and tilt it up and take a big gulp and swallow it all at once.

Sonney pulls the glass from my fingers and when I look up, feeling the cold beer spreading in my stomach and rising up through my nose at the same time, sharp as vinegar, he looks afraid.

"Omigod, Miller," he says, "I didn't mean for you to actually *take* a drink . . ."

"Why not, it don't taste all *that* bad," I say, and Sonney goes white.

Another song I've heard enough to remember comes on the jukebox:

"There's a star-spangled banner waving somewhere
In a distant land so many miles awa-a-y . . ."

"Sonney," John says soothingly, "it ain't necessarily 'like father like son,' Christamighty, he's just a kid . . . "

"I was thinking of Turner," Sonney says, shaking his head, looking almost sad enough to cry. "When I think what it cost Turner when he was on it, and then what it cost him to go off it, and here I am funnin' around with his boy. Jesus, I'm a stupid old fart . . ."

I wait for the verse I want:

"Lincoln, Custer, Washington and Per-ry . . ."

Then I join in and holler along with the song:

"*Nathan Hale and Colin Kelly too*!"

Chairs stir and scrape somewhere behind us and Sonney goes a little whiter and John Presley reaches out and taps him on the back of his thick wrist: "Sonney . . ."

Some beer-fizz rises up in my throat and I go, "ROARRK!"

My eyes water. "Jesus Christ," I say, "let's vote on that one!"

Sonney's still pale and doesn't seem to know what to do or say. "Merciful God," he breathes, opening and closing his big hands.

I feel good. I could probably learn to like beer if I worked at it. John Presley's still smiling so everything's okay. Then John's smile fades as he turns to Sonney and says, "Jesus, that was a damned shame about Colin Kelly, no two ways about it."

Chapter Two

Rex and I stood inside the cabin across the drive from the kitchen-dining room complex that ordinarily went to the head cook, but which Rex had commandeered for us. Or so I had thought.

" . . . so you can see how it'll work out better for the both of us if we split up as to cabins, Miller . . . I mean so's we each got a private place to go to in case there's anything happening . . . and if there ain't, well, what the hell, we'll come over later on, the two of us, and'll set around and drink beer and bullshit, fuck 'em all, y' know? No way we can lose on this one, either of us, hey? . . ."

"Yeah . . ." He'd been explaining why I should go over to four clumped help shacks about fifty feet away, none of them as desirable as the one in which we now stood, and stake out my claim early; how it'd be worth my while to get the southwest one, since it was the largest, most private, and had no adjoining doors like the other three. It sounded like good advice, but being relegated never set well with me and always made me feel a bit surly. But I didn't protest.

Behind the cabin in the shade of a young maple sat Rex's pride and joy, his gleaming pearl-gray '46 Ford Coupe, stock save for dual glasspacks: leaving it there with its grill leering toward the kitchen was like an advertisement.

Then Ardis Gray was outside, shrilling even as her knuckles tattooed the wood frame of the screen door: "Rex! Miller! I'm so glad you're here, boys, but let's *go*, I need me some *help*! Duane's here too! Between us all, we'll get it done . . ."

* * *

Like Rex and me, Duane Hedder was local, a seventeen-year-old who'd worked as pot washer last summer; Ardis Gray herself was local, a "swamprat," as the unkind might say of any of us. Ardis had been the Champs' pastry cook for twenty seasons and was by now a kind of institution at the place, so well-liked that guests and help alike didn't complain when her pies contained hard little bits of unsifted sugar.

Duane was elsewhere at the moment, Ardis told us; but he'd be there later to do the pots and pans while the three of us would handle the food end of the wedding operation; then Rex and I would do the dishes and mop the floor after tonight's buffet dinner.

Tomorrow, however, the wedding reception would be catered by an outfit from Traverse City: "That's so after breakfast us help can just relax and enjoy ourselves and think about Clover and Jeff and not about dirty dishes. Isn't that nice of Clover? She *insisted*!" Ardis came from Deer Rapids, two miles across the lake from the Champs as the crow flies, about eleven by car. In her early forties, she was short, rotund, shrill-voiced, but kindly; tight curls of crow-black hair shot with strands of gray were bunched like grapes over her forehead and at her temples. She beamed everywhere her adoration of the LaBaughs in general and Clover in particular.

Ardis was already in the aisle between the ranges and the serving and steam tables in the main part of the kitchen when we got there—it looked odd to see her there, diminutive and bustling. Ardis did not like meat and vegetable cooking but, like the rest of us, had been willingly dragooned for the occasion. I was certain she'd sooner have had a stroke than miss the Champs' event of this end of the century: for the wedding, like Clover LaBaugh herself, was a one-of-a-kind, once-in-a-lifetime kind of deal.

* * *

Wearing a long apron with ties brought around and knotted in front over a white T-shirt and jeans, I opened the swinging doors to the dining room and was startled to discover, instead of an empty lemon-smelling room with breezes fluttering curtains, a dozen or so people milling around expectantly, waiting to be waited upon: just like summer. A good number of them were old-timers, guests of years standing and friends of the LaBaughs—and as well most of the LaBaughs were there: Clover's mother ("the old gal" to the help), Etta LaBaugh, the matriarch, a benign-looking dumpy woman in her late fifties with large fish-flat blue eyes and gray hair that shone like platinum, stood by the drinks table in the center of the room, accepting congratulations and exchanging pleasantries with well-wishers while other family members—Gerald and Roy, Clover's older pear-shaped brothers and their wives and various children—hung about on the peripheries, chatting among themselves.

Clover's older sister, the severe and unpleasant Daphne LaBaugh Redpath (my judgment, based largely on demeanor), had yet to appear, nor had I yet seen Yvonne LaBaugh Goode, the middle sister.

When I'd first come into view, the assemblage had all looked quickly and expectantly at me, but when they saw I'd brought them nothing, was merely scullery help gawking, they continued their conversations.

On a table near the center of the pleasant dining room were many bottles of liquor of all sorts and a big cut-glass bowl of ice cubes. Most paused during lapses in conversation to take generous swallows from their generous drinks; the sound of tinkling ice was everywhere. Among the guests were several middle-aged couples: the Wendell Galaghers, the Sturgis Gilmores, the Millard Wahoolas (their daughter, Gloria Wahoola, in her late thirties, nicely filled out a provocative short dress with vertical white and blue stripes), the Milton Steiners, the Kent Carutherses; and representing the younger folk, keeping close to the laden table and drinking Budweiser from the bottle, were Donnie Redpath, Daphne's son, a sophomore from Auburn, and his inseparable pal and general straight man, lackey and Delta Tau Delta brother, a bulbous clown named Jack Tudd. They were both focussing eagerly on a thin, attractive young woman named Christy Bannerman, a cousin of Gloria Wahoola, who had spent a month at the resort last summer. They were not vying for her attention—Jack Tudd was clearly comfortable with his role as deferential second banana. Each time Donnie uttered some witticism, Jack Tudd broke into wheezy, sycophantish giggles that caused Christy to wrinkle her pretty nose and look at Donnie as if to ask: 'Why'd you bring this prick along?' Near Christy stood slender and shy-looking Bettina Lourde, Clover's maid of honor and roommate from the University of Michigan. She was following the conversation intently, but looked shyly away whenever eyes fell upon her.

The smorgasbord table was set up as for a Friday night during the summer season: aluminum pans on which to put hot dishes, a few chafing dishes with sterno going, awaiting potted victuals to be set into their frames, the red heat lamp suspended from the ceiling where the head cook carved rib roasts and steamship rounds at the smorgs. And here came Rex now, in checked cook's trousers and a highly starched tunic and chef's toque, carrying in a huge roasting pan a complete round of beef, probably fifty-five pounds or so, that Ardis would have started cooking at 300 degrees as much as twelve hours earlier so guests could get rare close to the bone that would be tender as a loin cut.

As soon as Rex set the hot pan on a wooden cutting board beneath the red lamp, the host set their drinks on their tables and headed for the hot meat, which Rex began to cut expertly and to order with a long, beef-slicing knife while Ardis kept an eye on things in the ovens and steam tables and served beverages. The haunch, smelling of garlic and rosemary, looked vast on the table. Blood oozed from fork punctures down its sides.

Ardis stepped through the swinging doors between kitchen and dining room and motioned to me.

I was to be the go-between who carried platters and chafing dishes out to the table and then took their ravaged predecessors back to the kitchen to re-supply and re-garnish.

While back in the kitchen, I also dipped shrimp in Drake's mix and dropped them into baskets in the fryers, then made several baskets of French fries for the demand created by the kids and younger folk; and as well made an urn of coffee, put on hot water for tea, and did any other scutwork that befell me.

During a lull, Rex disappeared and I went out and stood behind the steamship round next to Ardis, now wilted and dumpy, with dinnerplates of sweat under the arms of her white nylon uniform. The guests were all seated, eating, and to me, a depressing sight for no reason I could fathom.

Out of boredom I was about to turn and go back into the kitchen when I spotted Yvonne LaBaugh Goode, Clover's twenty-nine-year-old sister, coming through the main doors opposite me. She was a pleasant sight: I'd always liked her, and with more reason than I disliked her sister Daphne.

Yvonne was just about my height, five-seven, and standing before me in tweed skirt and sweater she looked the school teacher she was. I found myself hard put to keep my eyes off the swellings of breasts and hips—I had always thought her luscious, like a nearly over-ripe strawberry. I liked her from the start, and more so after our first little bit of commerce when I washed and waxed her red '55 T-Bird last summer. I was impressed when she'd come out and helped me work the last of the Simoniz off with a flannel cloth; she'd worked hard, concentrating on what she was doing, her arm muscles fluttering, breasts lifting beneath her over-sized green chamois-cloth shirt as she zeroed in on a bit of dried wax with a strong circular motion. She'd seemed interested, too, in my plans for college, and as we'd talked about her teaching I discovered she wrote short stories and had published several in literary magazines. I'd liked her so much and so quickly, and I reckon, without qualification because I didn't detect the slightest condescension in her and because I recognized in her one of Turner's most appealing qualities: down-to-earthness. No Bullshit. Out with it, straight from the chest: Say what you mean, mean what you say; or keep your mouth shut. Yvonne always looked you full in the eyes and concentrated on *you*, no matter what was happening nearby. She was dark-skinned and I'd spent long minutes last summer wondering: would I call her swarthy or tawny? (The latter, I decided, on the basis of sound.) Her hair was dark and thick and somewhere between wavy and curly. I imagined it to be wonderfully odorous, and yes, had imagined thrusting my nose into its curly mass and inhaling, the tip of my nose perhaps touching the cool rim of an ear. The word *smitten* had occurred to me then, and it returned to me now.

Yvonne advanced across the room, heading directly for me, eyes fixed on me all the way, smiling: "Why, hello, Miller, so *good* to see you and have you here among us again!" And took both my hands in hers, held them, squeezed them. "My *God* your hands are thick and strong—all that callus!—and I don't know why I'm greeting you like a long-lost friend, we've only been away from here a month—but there's just something about October, God isn't that a lovely sound, the most euphonious of the months, and by the time it rolls around everything's *so* different from summer mode, you know . . . it's *truly* my favorite month . . ."

"Yeah . . . mine too . . ." And so it was: going from September to October was like watching a shaken jar of muddy water clarify itself, a time that still partook of the summer but also anticipated November's somber gloom, And I couldn't help saying, "I like the light on trees then, especially birches and oaks, and the kind of hush in the woods, except for the little animals . . . 'course the damn hunters always come along and mess things up. Then there's the way the hills look in the distance . . ."

"Yes, and what always hits me strongly is the sense time's running out—it's October when you should step back from your life and see if there are changes you need to make, no matter whether you have the strength or will to effect said changes. Doesn't Rilke end 'Archaic Torso of Apollo' this way: 'You must change your life.'? Well, there I go again, parading my virtual *compulsion* for literary allusions, one of the few things I share with my erstwhile, ah, better half. Disregard that, Miller. Say, you look great, like you could whip your weight in the proverbial wildcats."

My throat felt dry, she was a little too close and I smelled her flowery perfume and felt an unwanted catch in my breathing and a buzzing in my groin. Last summer Yvonne'd asked me to demonstrate some basic weight-lifting exercises and I'd obliged her, using a broom handle, feeling her intent gaze upon me like summer sun in the gloom of the old icehouse across from the kitchen whose floor still smelled richly of the ancient sawdust in which ice used to be kept.

"Stick around and I'll show you my new car—and if it were summer I'd ask if you were available to Simoniz it."

"I'd be happy to anyhow," I said quickly, my voice sounding a bit unnatural in my ears. "I'll make time."

Yvonne reached over and pinched my cheek, then was gone, turning toward the group of friends and relatives moving to greet Clover and Jeff Budlong, who'd just come through the dining room's front door. And there behind Clover came Harrison Goode, Yvonne's husband, an English professor at Washington University in St. Louis, slender, bronzed, pushing forty, with thinning hair and a gray-striped suit with unpadded shoulders and narrow lapels—the "Ivy League" style. I wondered if as well there was one of those useless little belts at the back of his expensive trousers. His face was flushed, his eyes damp, and he had a highball glass in his hand—as he and Yvonne made eye contact, he raised it to his lips and chugalugged it like a can of beer. Yvonne bit her lip and looked at the floor, then turned to say something to Clover. Daphne LaBaugh Redpath's sharp gaze seemed locked on Professor Goode, who was usually called HG, with clear distaste.

Rex returned and as I moved away from his spot behind the smorg table, he murmured, "Looks like the professor's got an early start on getting shit-faced. And with a woman like that, what a waste, huh . . ."

He cast his eyes to the ceiling in something like pain at the cast-away possibilities and into my head shot the little caricature on *The Detroit News* funnies where Puck wore a banner proclaiming "What fools these mortals be!"

Ardis came over and stood beside me and we all regarded the LaBaugh "party," as we would have said in the summer: Clover LaBaugh and Jeff Budlong wearing jeans and Shetland sweaters, hand in hand; slender Jerry Smink, the best man, handsome and self-assured like the groom himself, save that his hair was reddish; Bettina Lourde; and like Tweedle Dee and Tweedle Dum,

Gerald and Roy LaBaugh, in their thirties and looking alike enough to be twins, bulbous and humorous as garlic cloves, their fat necks striated and latticed from the sun; and behind them all, Etta LaBaugh, sour-looking as a toad, leaning on her ebony cane; her vision was so poor without her glasses, which she refused to wear to dinner, that she doubtless perceived those over six feet away as blobs. Still, like someone blind who knows his way around his own property, you got the impression she probably didn't miss that much.

As we watched, I saw the group collectively realize they were being scrutinized by Rex and me and Ardis; and a kind of silent communication rippled through them and they all seemed to make almost a half turn in our direction and stand a little taller and straighter; Clover and Jeff began to smile slightly as if their picture were being taken; Jerry Smink straightened his shoulders; however, Etta LaBaugh, perhaps not sensing the scrutiny, or demonstrating her total indifference to it, kept scowling toward the west wall.

Only Yvonne and Harrison Goode seemed oblivious to being watched—they were looking into each other's faces and even a fool could tell they were locked in a state of contention.

Donnie Redpath seemed to have disappeared, as had Jack Tudd, and Christy Bannerman. We'd earlier glimpsed four or five other college age men and women, but they'd drifted away shortly after the makeshift buffet began.

Clover LaBaugh suddenly broke free from her party and came over to speak directly to the three of us: "Ardis! Rex! Miller! It's just *so* wonderful that you're here too to share the most wonderful time of my life! It wouldn't be the same without you!" Her eyes shone, her skin glowed, and she projected *noblesse oblige* without a hint of condescension, a true LaBaugh at her best.

Arrowhead

October 1957

It was a little before 7:00 and the sun was setting.

Doc Knowles and I sat across from one another under a twisted Jonathan tree of our gone-to-seed orchard behind and high up above our house and junkyard and outbuildings, both of us rooting in the dirt before us with our jack-knives where we'd created funnel-shaped excavations like giant ant-lion holes. We were near the spot where Doc had once found a beautifully-sculpted Ojibway pelt scraper, half a pound of flint with very sharp and delicately-flaked edges.

These days, Doc kept the tool in a footlocker in the attic, rather like the one Rex and I shared, where he and his younger brother Tucker lived, and he was surprisingly possessive about it—two years ago he'd refused the Ermine Falls School superintendent's request that he bring it to school for an exhibit on Indian things for fear of something befalling it, in spite of the super's assurances. He also resisted suggestions that he should give it to the Con Foster Museum in Traverse City, which had a substantial collection of Indian artifacts.

We'd probably raked through this area half a dozen times over the years, and at different seasons, but we'd never again made a decent find here since Doc's—just bits of flaked flint that'd apparently been discarded by the Indian craftsmen as unworthy, and a few bits of pottery and once half a clay pipe. And many traces of old fires.

Doc was home for a weekend from his first year at Central State University and was going on about the place where it seemed likely I'd end up too: "Yeah, it can be a lot of fun, Miller, though can't say's I like the bastards forcing me to take ROTC. But what the hell, everybody gets stuck with it. Organic chem's been hard for me and it's gonna take me a while to get up to handling calculus. There's lottsa' crap I have to take that I'll never have any practical need for as a vet, but what the hell . . ."

"How's the quiff situation?"

"Fine . . . that is if you got a car and money . . ."

"Yeah?"

"Yeah—come on down for a weekend sometime, you and Rex, we'll see what we can scare up . . ."

"Thanks, that's a thought . . ."

"How you doing with Ruth Ann?"

"Ah, I dunno . . . s'like a lot of boy-girl things, I guess, I want her but don't want to get pulled into any kind of permanent thing—meanwhile, she wants me too, but not if it's something less than kind of permanent . . ."

"Yeah, well, I—hey! Got a bite here!" He stuck his hand deep into the hole he'd been excavating, pulled out a flat dark object, and tossed it so it landed with a damp plop on the ground before me.

"Hey," I said, "by now this could be likely a kind of artifact—it's an old pack of Luckies, look it's got a green pack, 'member that one, 'Lucky Strike Green Has Gone to War'—they claimed they used the green pigment for making bronze needed for bearings in tanks, so they turned to white and red packs . . .probably all bullshit . . ."

"Yeah, think I sort of remember . . ." Doc and I were about the same age. Again I wondered about Turner's judgment in keeping me out of school until I was seven.

"Here." I gave the cold, sodden pack an underhand flick back over to him: "Check to see if there's anything inside, maybe somebody hid a ten dollar bill in it, y' never know . . ."

"Hmmm . . . just nothing but a soggy old pack and two totally fucked-up cigarettes . . . probably no point offering this one up to the Con Foster museum . . ."

My knife was edging around a rock or something and I crammed the point deeper in the dirt around it, then pried it up with my fingers until it came loose.

I pulled it up, and without looking, cocked my arm to send it hurtling over into the darker reaches of the orchard.

But something stopped me: the sharp edge of what I'd figured was a chunk of shale reminded me of something, the sharp minutely-serrated edge of Doc's flensing tool.

I lowered my arm, brought the object close and even before I saw it clearly I could feel from its flat surfaces that it wasn't shale and its pits didn't come from aeons of dripping water and abrading stones—a human hand had flaked the arrowhead.

"Whatcha got there?" Doc asked.

"Dunno, I'm trying to see . . ." I took my bandanna from my hip pocket, spat on the arrowhead and rubbed off the black earth, spat on it again, then wiped it again and held it up—there was still enough light to see by, though it was fading fast. "Jesus," I murmured.

It was the equal of Doc's find in craftsmanship, and the finely made edges were so beautifully done that I wondered if it might have been made by the same craftsman as Doc's piece.

Doc's piece was ordinary gray and white flint while this one was black and white and gray, the streaks running longitudinally.

I looked up at Doc and tossed it to him.

He let out a low whistle: "Christ, this's a beauty. And we thought your orchard was played out. Want to sell it?"

"No," I said instantly. "Maybe later, but I want to have it for a while just to look at and turn it over in my hands . . . doesn't seem like something I should own, at least not for very long . . ."

"How come?"

"I don't know . . . it's . . . just *feels* like it'd be wrong for me to have it for very long, but I sure can't bring myself to put it back in the ground and leave it either . . ."

I thought Doc'd tell me I was crazy, but he nodded like he understood—and maybe he did. He used to collect butterflies when he was a kid but quit because he couldn't square his love for the things with having to kill them for his collection.

"Or who knows, maybe I'll show it to Turner and ask him what he thinks later on," I said as the curved edge of sun eased below the horizon and plunged the orchard into a comforting semi-darkness. "He'll know what ought to be done with it. But I want to own it myself for a little while . . ."

That solved, clutching my find tightly in my left hand, I flopped on my back beside my little excavation. Eight or ten feet away, Doc did the same and we lay there in the dim orchard looking up at a bright crescent of new moon that had begun to assert itself as soon as the light began to fail: no longer the lacy, barely visible wisp afloat in the blue skies of day, it now looked shooting-star bright.

Chapter Three

Later, sometime after 8:00, the LaBaugh's and their guests rose en masse and drifted graciously from the dining room to whatever pastimes were planned for evening (or perhaps nothing was: perhaps all would simply flow spontaneously toward wherever seemed appropriate or interesting at any given moment). In any event, they'd certainly have to find a new location: their tables were now cluttered and disheveled and the smorg table itself was a shambles strewn with gobbets of food.

Ardis, pleading fatigue, left for her cabin to "freshen up"—which meant she'd pretty much exhausted her daily allotment of energy and wouldn't be back until we served breakfast in the morning: so Rex and I confronted work (for which we were getting, after all, $1.25 an hour; we kept scrupulous track of our hours).

The pot and pan sink at the west end of the kitchen was cluttered with a mountain of encrusted and scrofulous pots, pans, skillets and aluminum trays. Ten feet of counter leading up to the antiquated Jackson dishwasher were piled with a precarious assembly of dishes, cups, glasses, and silverware. Duane came in silently, nodded to us, pulled on an oilcloth apron and heavy black gloves, doffed his glasses, and bleakly began attacking the junk in the pot sink amid rising clouds of steam.

Sighing, we pulled on old blue rubber gloves still astink with last summer's sweat. Rex tossed a spoonful of soap into the machine, slammed the door on a flat tray of semi-soaked silverware and punched the button; I began scraping refuse from dishes into a hole in the counter that emptied into a garbage can beneath, then slamming them into trays for washing. It'd likely take us until around 9:30 or 10:00 by the time we finished policing everything up, considering that we'd promised Ardis we'd mop the kitchen floor as well. To make the prospect more palatable, I'd earlier resolved to take a swim when I was done no matter what the time or what the temperature of Lake Albion—I felt a strong yearning for the sharp, clear unambiguous thrill of heart-stopping cold water.

* * *

The stink of floor compound, mop water and rubber gloves clung to me; I'd retained my eagerness for the lake through all the filthy work, and back in my cabin I shucked off my clothes and kicked them under the bunk.

I looked at myself naked in the bureau's mirror, grinned, gave my image the finger, flexed my biceps, spread my lats, tightened my abdominals: not bad, who'd've guessed I was called Runt in my early grades?

I got into my nylon trunks, pulled my hooded sweatshirt on, grabbed a towel I'd cadged from the laundry and tossed it over my shoulder. I stuck a small unwrapped guest's bar of Ivory into the handwarmer pocket and was out the door, exhilarated at the prospect of jumping out into the dark over the water, of that lovely moment of suspension just before I hit the surface. It felt good to be alone. Rex was who knew where and Duane had gone to his home three miles away—so far it looked as though I mightn't have a single neighbor in my cabin complex. Certainly Donnie and Jack Tudd weren't going to be there.

I sauntered past the deserted kitchen. The night was clear and there were plentiful stars by whose light I could easily find my way. I recalled there'd been a new moon for several days, so likely tomorrow or the next day we'd see the beginnings of a crescent, perhaps one that would reveal the outline of the dark moon itself.

Inside the kitchen the lights blazed gaily on. Soon the floor would be dry, but I decided against coming back later and putting down the chairs and stools and other things Rex and I'd put on counters when we mopped—that could wait until morning.

Unless something occurred to dissuade or distract me, I'd head back to my cabin after swimming with a sandwich made from the round of beef and read Chekhov until I fell asleep. I was about to begin *The Kiss*, which Doc had recommended. And maybe I'd read some more Marvell in my renaissance poetry book: "The grave's a fine and private place/But none I think do there embrace" alone was enough to make my hair stand on end.

Past the kitchen, I followed the drive down to the lodge. The cool cement felt good on my bare soles, and I wriggled my shoulders in the ample folds of sweatshirt.

Across from the lodge and facing the kitchen was a parking area sufficient for seven or eight cars. I spotted two identical Cadillacs side-by-side, one gray and one the color of blueberries, a chocolate '57 Ford two-door station wagon, and a resplendent turquoise and white '57 two-door Chevy that looked rakish and devil-may-care next to the somber elegance of the Caddies and cheerless Ford.

"That's mine, Miller, what do you think?"

I turned. Yvonne LaBaugh, shrouded in a dark robe that ran from her chin to her ankles emerged from in the shadows of the hemlock behind me. She held a highball glass with tinkling ice in one hand and when she saw me regarding it she said, "Merely tonic and ice and water and a little lime, Miller, I don't know if you remember from summer but I drink only on special occasions . . . for reasons you can perhaps guess." She looked—I followed her glance—at her gleaming two-tone '57 Chevy. "Whaddaya think? Neat, huh? It's my 'heavy Chevy,' as my students call it."

Yvonne did a little pirouette and as her dark robe bulged and sagged from the movement of her body, I recalled a line from Sir Philip Sidney: "She even in black doth make all beauties flow."

"Neat," I said, swallowing hard. "Although since I remember your '55 T-Bird, I'm surprised you didn't get something like, say, a Studebaker Golden Hawk, or a Corvette. How's Mister Goode like it?"

"Well, aren't you perceptive—I think. Hmmmm. No, I truly loved my T-Bird, Miller, but I just didn't want to project such a racy persona anymore—but I wanted something bright and perky, if you know what I mean. In any case, this is *all* mine and that perfectly hideous Ford wagon parked there is all HG's. It's supposed to be *mocha*! God, how drab. At any rate, we came all the way from St. Louis in separate cars, need I say more? God! Are we really all this remote from our youth? Answer: I guess so. A few minutes ago I went down to the lodge and they were getting ready to have a kind of merry little sing-along around the piano, and when I suggested we all of us go skinny-dipping like we once did, well, at least twice when we were in our teens back in the late forties and used to waitress here, Daphne and Gloria Wahoola and June Belding anyhow, they all just looked *totally* askance, scandalized, all mature and huffy and outraged, not to mention white and sedentary and out of shape—too timid to jump in the water when it's this cold: in short, like *oldsters*! My God!"

"I'll go swimming with you if you want," I said, horrified as the words popped out, each in my imagination like half a morel mushroom strung on a piece of string to dehydrate; then, as my pulse began to accelerate, I thought giddily of my sentence as a long strand of spaghetti that I'd like suck back in my mouth: but couldn't.

Yvonne turned, regarding me speculatively; then she tossed her highball glass off into the dark in the general direction of the kitchen (from our present vantage, its variety of lights made it look like some hulking galleon tethered to a dock) and reached out and took my hand—hers was wet and cold from gripping the icy glass and strong and supple as a trout lifted up from a livebox. "Let's go," she said, "although be aware I'm acting on the idea that, as someone once said, p'raps it was Oscar Wilde, 'If it's worth doing, it's worth doing badly . . .'" She pulled me across the drive and out of the light, then dropped my hand and left me to follow as she swished forward in her dark shape-shifting robe, moving sinuously in the semi-dark toward the waterfront.

She called back over her shoulder: "If my heart should seize up from the shock of the water, please just forsake me: I don't wish to be resuscitated."

"The same goes for me, too," I called after her, and for a moment I was struck by a vision of ourselves drowned together, slack bodies slipping and sliding over dark slippery pieces of driftwood on the lake bottom, our lifeless eyes inches above clam trails.

Arrangement in Gray and Black

April 1958

When Rex was discharged from the army in April of 1958, he took a series of buses from New Jersey. Turner and I met him at the Greyhound station in Traverse City when he came in on a Tuesday at 6:15 PM.

Rex wore new jeans and loafers and a light windbreaker over a bright white shirt that still had creases from the box. He smiled, moved stiffly, and looked a little disoriented when he stepped off the bus, as if he were surprised at finding himself, finally, back home. Perhaps it was a day he'd looked forward to, but when it actually arrived it was so different from what he'd thought or hoped it would be that it left him a little shaken.

For the first couple of days at home, too, he seemed dazed, as if he still questioned the fact that he really *had* come home, that he wasn't on leave and would never have to return to the army.

"Take her slow, let him ease back into things," Turner advised. "He's not going to be near as fucked up as me when I got back from the war, but he's been a far piece and . . . there needs to be a spell where for a while don't nobody rock the boat . . ."

It seemed to work. After a couple of days of doing some work back in the yard with Turner removing rebuildable truck transmissions from wrecks, Rex began to look a little more like his old self again. We all began to follow our old routines of when we got up and ate, worked and did chores, and on Friday Rex and Turner went off to an auction in Lansing with the flatbed truck and brought home a late model Pontiac wreck. Meanwhile, I went off to school as usual, taking along Sinclair Lewis's *Babbitt* for slack moments.

It took Rex until Friday evening before he went to check over his '46 Ford Coupe, the thing I'd thought he'd go for first. He took that slow, too. Inspected it carefully. Installed a new battery on Saturday and changed the oil, then drove it out of the barn and up by the shop, where he washed it. He waxed it on Sunday, declining my offer of help. But then he didn't seem to have much of an idea where he might want to go so I suggested we go see Sonney and Pearl MacReady in the evening. They'd been our substitute parents while Turner was at the war, and we knew they'd be wanting badly to see him.

"They got television yet?" Rex had asked, moving a toothpick around in his mouth.

"Nah . . . Sonney says they don't want it, says they'd sooner just listen to the radio . . ."

Rex grinned tentatively. "Ain't this the night for 'Our Miss Brooks' and 'Jack Benny' and 'The Great Gildersleeve' and 'Edgar Bergen and Charlie McCarthy'? They still on the radio?"

"Well, I kinda think they're most of them on TV now. I haven't listened to the radio much myself lately . . ."

"Jesus, it's been a while," Rex said wonderingly. "Y' know, I'm almost afraid to go see them because they were looking older than usual when I was home at Christmas—remember how it used to seem to us like they'd never change?"

* * *

We walked the mile and a quarter down Michigan 115 to their place instead of going in Rex's coupe. It was sort of like when we were kids staying with the MacReady's during the war and we walked most everywhere except for the once or twice a week Sonney drove his Model A pickup into town for one thing or another, sometimes for us to sell our onion sacks of milkweed pods to Guilder's store, where they'd go to make life jackets for aviators and sailors. We were saving up for a Savings Bond.

"Feels kinda good walking this way again," I said. The air was clear and cool and the setting sun was at our backs.

"Yeah, and it feels good to be walking for yourself and not nobody telling you to walk here, walk there, and how fast and how far and when to take a drink and a piss . . ."

"Turner's sure glad you're back."

We walked on in silence. Rex's difference, even though I could feel and see it dissipating before my eyes, still made me a little wary. He looked happy without me trying to make conversation so I kept my mouth shut.

* * *

Together we stepped up on the MacReady's sagging, unpainted stoop and the ancient boards flexed so deeply I was afraid for a moment we were going to plunge through them like two Rumplestiltskins.

Before we could knock, Pearl jerked the screen door open and stood there smiling idiotically, wanting to throw her arms about Rex but also wanting to see him whole.

When she'd locked this first view of him into memory, she pressed up against him and put her arms around him. Just behind her stood Sonney, leaning on his cane, face split by a deep grin. They were both in their seventies now. Pearl was bone thin, wrinkled, the sharp white and pink of her dentures a surprise in her seamed face; and Sonney, tough as nails still, was bent like a dying tree. Now he relied on his cane instead of using it mostly as a prop or tool.

Pearl and Rex kept hugging, he patting her over and over on her bent back, she talking softly and quickly— "It's so *good*, Rex, to see you, just so *good*, I tell you there was a time in January when we wasn't sure we'd be here for the return of the Prodigal Son . . . but it's really you, and you're here, and we're here and everything seems kind of back to normal, leastways for a little bit . . ."

Sonney could no longer contain himself: "You fellers see what *ain't* here no more as you come up?"

Pearl loosed Rex and we all three looked at him, Pearl shaking her head as if to say '*That man*.' Rex and I were mystified.

"The shop!" Sonney crowed. "It ain't there no more, that's our big news . . . we sold it to Doctor Kittridge in Skeegemog—he had a whole crew come out here and they took it all apart in a day and carted the boards off and then they come back and hauled away all the crap, the rotted floor joists and like that . . . give us three hundred dollars, fellers, so now we kinda got us a little nest egg, been thinking on getting some insulation in 'fore winter and some other things, might get us a television, then you fellers could come down to see Ed Sullivan and Milton Berle, though I don't much care for it myself. Y' know, with them radio programs you had to put it together in your head, what the people looked like and what they're doing and how they are, but when they do it all for you in pictures on the screen you don't do nothing but set there and take it all in. And it ain't nothing like them rip-roaring Roy Rogers and Gene Autry westerns the four of us used to see to Skeegemog 'bout every other week during the war . . ."

Rex and I dutifully went back out and stood on the perilous stoop again. Where the shop had been, a modest wooden outbuilding where Sonney had his forge and tools and had done blacksmithing up until a decade ago, was nothing. He'd sold the forge itself and accompanying tools five years earlier. Now quackgrass sprouted from a square of raw-looking dirt where the building had been. Sonney's barn was still there, though, weathered to silver, but structurally sound and looking much as it did in the 1913 photograph of it and Sonney and his team of mules that I had at home.

"Doc Kittridge's going to panel his office and study with them good ole unwarped heavy-as-hell oak and some of them nice hickory boards like can't nobody find anymore for love nor money . . ."

Looking at the paucity where a familiar object had been, I felt half-sick, thinking of times I sat in there on the floor amid flying sparks as Sonney sharpened some farm tool, riding his grinder like a bicycle, which it somewhat resembled. Rex looked a little perplexed as well. He spoke first: "Well, that's just . . . great, Sonney, Christ knows you folks deserve a little ease . . ." I thought he was going to add "in your golden years," but he didn't. He smiled and I followed him back into the familiar room and we filled our lungs again with the homely scents of camphor, Baume Bengue, body odor, fuel oil, cooking spices.

* * *

Pearl brought out our favorite oatmeal and raisin cookies on the clear eye-blue platter that had belonged to her mother, and instead of the lemonade she usually made we had cold bottles of Coca-Cola. After they'd quizzed Rex for another ten minutes or so, it was time. Sonney turned on the huge old console, the familiar green tuning eye came on, and Rex and I lay on our backs on the rug with a cushion under each of our heads. We'd spent many hours thus during the war years when we lived with the MacReady's in a tiny but snug bedroom in the back of the house.

The radio warmed up, but there was no Jack Benny and Rochester and Phil Harris and Dennis Day and Mary Livingston and Don Wilson as on Sundays during the war. Instead, we listened to music on a station Sonney kept the console tuned to continuously, except when he wanted to hear the news, a classical music station.

He'd turned it on in the middle of something, piano music that splashed over us and spread to the corners of the room and made me think of raccoons washing something to eat in a stream, and then I thought how I should be glad Sonney and Pearl had come by a few bucks for something they didn't need any more, how I should rejoice rather than take the loss of that old building personally: what would I have them do, preserve it as a shrine?

The piece came to an end and the deep-voiced host told us we'd been listening to Mozart's Piano Concerto in F Major as the day's last light faded. The program would conclude with Chopin's Nocturnes 18 and 19, played by Arthur Rubinstein.

This somber yet somehow glad music seemed to require nothing from us save our presence as it wafted through the dark while we sat wordless, no one moving to turn on a light.

During the war years, Rex and I had always felt wanted and loved here, had always been warm and dry and well-fed. Living with a pitcher pump in the kitchen sink, no insulation, a single oil heater in the living room, and a privy out back whose ammoniac tang stung your eyes when you were ten feet away had seemed very natural. Now the MacReady's had an electric pump and faucets where the pitcher pump had been, and in the kitchen a 40-gallon propane-fired water heater; and an indoor toilet with a shower occupied half the room that had been our bedroom during the war.

"Them boards," Sonney said with a quaver during the space after the first Nocturne ended, "you can't get no more—they was over half well-seasoned oak planks and the rest was hickory of the sort that ain't to be had 'cept offa old buildings like ours . . . and now it's gone!" Tendons stood out in his neck, then he sought his cane and got up out of the chair and headed for the bathroom, as in years past he'd have headed outside for the privy.

Nocturne 19 commenced.

Rex and I continued to lie on the floor, loose and comfortable against one of Pearl's thick braided rag rugs. Sonney and Pearl sat in their customary rockers and at the conclusion of Nocturne 19 a quiet joy suffused us: what had been disrupted by necessities of one kind or another was now knit back together. For now, we had found a little pocket of time when we were all safe and together again.

* * *

Before we left, Sonney told me he had a shoe from one of his mules for me. I knew at once I'd make it a companion piece to the photograph he'd given me of himself and his team and barn in January of 1913, with a limber Sonney standing proudly before his newly-built barn holding the reins to Jenny and Maud.

During the war years he'd told Rex and me tales of Jenny's and Maud's prowess and steadfastness, their surefootedness and endurance: "So where'd they *go*?" I used to ask him. "What *happened* to them? They can't be alive *now*, can they?"

"No," he'd say. "Not exactly." And he'd gaze off into space.

"So how'd they die?" My curiosity had been enormous.

Sonney'd sigh and say, "Y' know, Miller, I like to think of the two of 'em knee-deep in pastures of clover, just like Old Faithful." He was referring to what Pearl, highly amused and gratified by our duets, used to call "our song."

"So did Maud and Jenny get put out to pasture when their working life was over so all they had to do was enjoy things until they was just so old they died in their sleep and then were buried right there in them clover pastures?"

"We all of us get out to pasture, Miller," he'd say vaguely, bringing the conversation to a close. Or he'd tell again how, when they were all young, he and Jenny and Maud could plow a row by eye as straight as if it'd been laid out by a plumb line.

* * *

He handed me a rusted mule shoe that he'd made himself and had once nailed onto a hoof of either Jenny or Maud.

"Thanks a lot, Sonney, I'm real glad to have this. I'll keep this where I got some other keepsakes, and whenever I take it out and hold it in my hand like this I'll think about you and me and Maud and Jenny, even if I never knew them . . ."

His eyes glistened; he was unable to answer.

Before we left, Sonney handed Rex a new scout-type jack-knife— "Figured the army might not've given you one, or maybe you lost your own . . ." —and Pearl without a word gave me a clean new envelope addressed to me and made me promise not to open it until I got home. I felt uncomfortable, knowing how generous they both were, and feared it might contain money; but I didn't seem to have much choice in the matter.

"Bye, fellers," Pearl said from the stoop as we left, "you all come on back real soon . . . maybe another Sunday just like this one if you can put up with us old folks again . . ."

Sonney didn't utter a word, but he lifted a trembling, benedictory hand.

Pearl called out as we moved off into the night: "Them war

years was wonderful 'cause of you boys! I know you come to us through trouble, but you boyses being with us was the best tonic we coulda *ever* had! And Miller, them duets you and Sonney used to sing was the best I ever heard!"

* * *

"Your ass!" I said to Rex on the way home at a little before ten. "They're just about like they was when you was home over Christmas, I—"

"Miller . . . Christ, that's because you *been* here all the while I was away and you don't see changes that happen just a little bit at a time. Sonney's hands didn't used to shake like that, Pearl didn't have to use her cane to get herself up out of the chair, Sonney didn't have that gimpy kinda walk he's got now . . . he didn't used to *need* his goddamned cane . . ."

* * *

Against a wall in our attic I'd set up a folding card table a few years back as a desk for my homework. Now I sat before it on my fold-up chair beneath a 60-watt bulb hanging from a ceiling joist as Rex undressed to crawl into his bunk next to mine at the far end of the attic. I propped the picture Sonney had given me against my cigar box of odds and ends: Jenny and Maud, in full harness and blinders, stood before the barn, and there was Sonney himself, holding the reins, strong and youthful, wiry, ready for anything.

I pulled the mule shoe Sonney'd given me closer: against its narrow wishbone symmetry an ordinary plow horse shoe looked fat and clumsy. This one bore indentations from Sonney's hammer when he'd forged it, probably in the first decade of the twentieth century. The striker on the front had been worn down by use, and one of the rectangular four-nail holes on one side was plugged. I stuck the end of a paper clip through it and a bit of dried dirt fell onto the tabletop. I wet a forefinger, touched it to the crumbs of earth, then put them on my tongue, feeling the grit against my teeth. How long had that soil lain there? How long since Sonney'd removed this shoe from Maud or Jenny, then reshod her? In its own way the shoe was as much a thing of beauty as Gracious Carstairs' Cries of London plates from which Doc and Tucker and Welles Stringer and Larry Carstairs and I had eaten cake and ice cream a decade ago on Larry's birthday.

I put the shoe aside and opened the envelope Pearl had given me, and was relieved when no cash fell out. There were two letters, one on a small sheet of cheap lined notebook paper, the other on a yellowing sheet of typing paper.

The first was written on the day I was born.

Ermine Falls, Mich
June 20 1939

Miller Stephen Springstead: —Dear Little Friend:—

We welcome you and rejoice that you have come among us and be a great pleasure to your parents, and we know you will be a blessing to them all through your life for yours will be a useful and helpful life, we are so anxious to see you and be with you, we know you and us will be great friends.

We are wishing you a long-long life and a happy life.

We are your friends with love to you

—Sonney and Pearl MacReady.

The second was written to me, and it was from Sonney and dated June 1945; I recognized Pearl's writing—probably she had made a copy before Sonney sent me the original:

"My Dear little Miller can't you Come Down and Help me Hoe the weeds out of the Berries Before picking time. you Know We have great times. a. c. MacReady Love to you Auntie Pearl said to tell you to come Down we Had something for you goodby"

* * *

I thought now of when Sonney and I had sung "Old Faithful" together, and how our duet always gave Pearl such pleasure she could never stop smiling as we sang, Sonney in a melodious baritone, on key, me with my piping kid voice:

"Old Faithful, we rode the range together,
Old Faithful, in every kind of weather . . .
When your roundup days are over
There'll be pastures wide with clover
For you, Old Faithful pal o' mine . . ."

I let my head down on the flimsy surface of the cardtable and gasped in a spasm of anguish that was close to weeping but wasn't. I felt a dry, surly contorting of my features I wouldn't want anyone to see. I kept tasting the earth from the muleshoe.

As soon as the fit was over, I reached back in my jeans, got out my bandanna and blew my nose.

As I sat there looking at the photograph of Sonney, and Jenny and Maud on January 11, 1913, Rex's voice, low and sad, sounding like Turner's, floated through the dark: "Don't worry, pal, they're tough old birds, they got some miles left in 'em, you'll see, we'll spend some more time with them . . ."

I didn't answer. I was too tired. And I was busy singing the last lines from "Old Faithful" in my head:

"Hurry up old feller,
We gotta get home tonight . . ."

Chapter Four

"How sweetly flows, / That liquefaction of her clothes"—that fragment from Sir Phillip Sydney came to me as I followed Yvonne, moving swiftly ahead of me through the gloom, her bare feet going *pat-pat-pat* as she descended the twenty feet or so of wooden steps that led down to the "help's dock"—so-called because during the season, employees were relegated to it and forbidden the more expansive and diving board-equipped "guest" dock (unless a help should be making arrangements for some appropriate task like washing a guest's car, cleaning fish, hauling fireplace wood, etc.).

This dock was more secluded than the guests', exposed as it was only to a single side of the boathouse overlooking the harbor; anyone approaching on the wooden stairs would announce himself well in advance. Atop the boathouse sat the pavilion, a large room with a hardwood dance floor, a couple of ping-pong tables and an old upright piano; during the summer it was the scene of much merriment as the democratizing element of drink brought guests and help together in sometimes interesting combinations. Its interior walls were lined with padded benches and, ordinarily by early October, the pavilion would have been filled with wooden swings, dock chairs, paddleboards and other Champs equipment.

And now, ragged boogie-woogie descended to us, a drubbing eight-to-the-bar bass against which a series of discordant chords snarled and grated. The windows were lit like the eyes of a jack-o'-lantern and glancing up toward the racket, Yvonne and I could see shadows cast on the pavilion ceiling but not the figures casting them. Even if the partiers looked out the windows and down at the dock, they wouldn't be able to see much of us, it occurred to me.

Yvonne took my elbow in her hand, turning me slightly north, and I managed to quell the impulse to jerk as though a bee'd stung me: "If you look way along the shore there to the point and then lift your eyes up you can sort of see the outline of what I've always called the 'promontory' . . . there, you see, where the lip of the bank kind of curls over on itself? There's a little grove of cedars set back from it and when I was a little girl—even as a teen-ager—I used to crawl back into the inner part of the grove where there's a little sort of bower and I'd sit there by myself at night, hugging my knees . . . it had a sort of cathedral feeling inside, there with the trees sort of leaning protectively in yet letting you see the stars and moon too . . ."

"*Yaiii-eeeeee*!" someone screamed in the pavilion above. Then, "*Yaii-eee*! *Yai-eeeeee*!" over and over—of course it would be Donnie Redpath, who went to Auburn and claimed he was an honorary southerner, demonstrating his rebel yell.

I wondered where Rex was, but only briefly since I'd a few other things on my mind.

I pulled my sweatshirt over my chest and shoulders and when my head popped free, I saw Yvonne, dark robe at her feet like a pool of oil, poised in her black two-piece, on tiptoes, eyes closed. I relaxed a little—so her chatter about skinny-dipping had been inflated. Or perhaps the proximity of her nephew and fellow roisterers brought her back to reality: either way, probably just as well.

Yvonne brought her arms behind her and tore open her top from behind and dropped it (sudden white globes, dark spots in their centers! No more than a yard away!), then shucked her bottom down so it was around her knees by the time the top hit the dock, then stepped daintily—and fast! Fast!—out of the circle made by the bottom and, a flash of black and gray and white, executed a flat graceful dive from the dock, the dark triangle where her legs joined still detonating in my head from my split-second glimpse before she'd become airborne.

She slipped graceful as a needle just beneath the water's surface, then came up for air, gasping from the cold, spitting water and tossing her head so a corolla of droplets rained around her like a handful of tossed birdshot.

"Last one in's a rotten egg!" Yvonne called in a soft chiding and challenging voice. "No room left at the inn for candy-asses!"

She was right, this was no time to dilly-dally: I rammed my trunks down over the impediment of my tire-iron stiff prick and hurled myself gracelessly into that void I'd been anticipating for hours.

Christ! it was cold!—like an open-handed smack in the face only all over your body. I was momentarily half-paralyzed by the water's coldness, had never felt anything like it before.

Then my limbs began to work and I dog-paddled madly to get my circulation going, then went underwater, wriggling, stroking with everything I had.

When I surfaced and shook my head, gulping air, I found Yvonne treading water, facing me with an enormous grin (what splendid white teeth she had): "*Ka-Splooosh*!" her hand skimmed a stinging cascade into my face; I swallowed some water and gasped, choked and emitted a strangled sound more a demented cackle than a laugh.

But I swallowed it down quickly and suddenly our faces were no more than a foot apart as we trod water, panting.

"God, what am I coming to—next I'll be accused of trying to . . . *intrigue* teen-agers . . . among my many other low crimes and high misdemeanors . . ."

"Well, I'm a teen-ager and I gotta admit I'm intrigued," I managed, shuddering in the freezing water, eliciting Yvonne's exciting throaty laugh before she turned and swam rapidly away from me in a smooth synchronized crawl toward the dock, where she briskly and noisily hoisted the composition in black, white and gray that was her naked body onto the weathered dock boards—again that black triangle surrounded by white which was in turn surrounded by a lesser darkness, again but for a split-second! She quickly slipped into her heavy dark robe, then stooped and retrieved her suit, stuffing its parts into her robe's oversized pockets.

And now, swaddled from throat to ankles in her voluminous robe, arms folded, Yvonne stood surveying me like the spectator she'd suddenly become, me, bare-ass in the frigging water with no other prospect save clambering awkward and naked onto the dock, doubtless giving her a splendid gander at me and what an authority like Rex would surely have deemed a blue-steeler.

I thought of the ever-canny Doc Knowles: What would he suggest in such a circumstance? (Easy, and it wouldn't take him forever either: "*Brazen it out! Miller, getchur naked ass on up there!*")

There was no way to slither inconspicuously across the dock and wrap my towel around me, all the while keeping my groin out of sight. So a mere yard from where Yvonne's feet were, I hoisted myself until my arms were straight, then spun around so my wet ass smacked smartly against the splintery boards and I sat facing away from her, concealing my affliction—at least for the moment.

When I stood I couldn't not turn, so I did, aware as I faced Yvonne of my cold-shriveled balls and my tingling cock swinging in the night air like a weathervane: and Yvonne stepped into me, pressing me close against the thick material of her robe, not shrinking as my prick pushed hard into the thick material a little below where her belly button would be, an area which instead of yielding in some pneumatic way pressed back. "Well, hello there, Intrigued." Then she pushed me to arm's length, and paying no observable attention to my nakedness and condition, turned away from me.

I quickly pulled my trunks and then my sweatshirt on—By the time I got my drawstring cinched and my towel wrapped firmly around my waist she was already to the end of the dock and about to begin climbing the stairs leading past the pavilion. I padded rapidly after her.

"*Thumper!*" someone screamed above us in the pavilion, bringing Yvonne to so abrupt a halt that I caught up to her in a few strides.

We listened side by side as the fists from the eight or ten people I guessed were involved madly hammered the hardwood floor. They abruptly ceased when someone screamed, "*Rex!*" "*Rex!*" echoed another. "You missed it, Rex! You fucked up! That's Jack Tudd's sign! Drink'r up, Rex, 'r drinker down, who cares!"

There was silence for a few moments, then another voice, half-choked, cried: "*Thumper*!"

Again the tattoo of fists on the floor, again the sudden cessation. "*Jack*!" someone screamed: "Jack Tudd! Rhymes with Pud! That's *Christy's* sign—she's got the *ear*-tug, not the *nose*-pull! You dummy!"

Yvonne and I ascended the stairs quickly and slipped furtively past the stairway leading to the pavilion's front door. I didn't like imagining Rex sitting on the floor with that bunch of college assholes playing Thumper, and I hated the thought of him getting smashed and losing his usual grace and suppleness, perhaps finding himself unable to keep straight what signs were whose: surely they'd snooker him, he of the relatively small capacity for booze.

Still, he'd chosen to go solo this operation so he'd have to deal with it, I had my own concerns at the moment.

"Donnie, brother Delt," cried a high-pitched voice, probably Jack Tudd's, "how's about a buncha roas' beef sanwidges? You got the in with the management, ain'tcha? You're an heir to this place, ain'tcha? *Woo-wooo*, *chugga-chugga*! *Yai-eeeeeee*!"

* * *

When we got up to the lodge Yvonne reached out and touched my forearm. "I'll be back in a minute, so don't go 'way, Intrigued . . . why don't you just lurk here back in the shadows and I'll be back in . . . two shakes of a lamb's tail . . ."

She entered the door to the small apartment Sheldon Renfrew occupied during the summer but which was Yvonne's and Harrison's for the wedding and disappeared into the dark. I heard her pause before shutting the screen door. And then I did step over onto the back porch of the lodge and press back against the wall so I stood in a column of black.

As I stood wondering if Yvonne'd be back in minutes or maybe up to an hour, or maybe not at all, I heard someone coming along the walk. I remained motionless and watched Donnie

Redpath lurching along, jauntily hoisting a beer bottle to his lips. On he went, splay-rooted, huge penny loafers slapping on the concrete walk, heading toward the kitchen.

As soon as Donnie disappeared, Yvonne stepped out the door—I doubted she'd been inside for much more than a couple of minutes. I wondered if she'd simply let fall her robe, then pulled on the khaki shorts and blue shaker-knit sweater she now had on, then stepped confidently into her sandals before turning back into the night to meet—me!

"Hello again, there, Intrepid. Or Intrigued. Or both. Do I take you're ensconced in a help's cabin?"

"Yeah . . ."

"*Alone*?" Her brows arched; they were glossy in the starshine.

"Yeah . . ."

"Well, let's go there . . ."

"Sure . . . let's . . ."

As we walked, close but not quite brushing, I did all the math I could: Lessee, I'm nineteen, I know Yvonne's either twenty-eight or twenty-nine, that's ten years . . . she was ten years old when I was an infant. For a moment I wished fervently I were a freshman in college instead of a mere senior in high school: Turner, why'd you have to keep me back that year?

We came up to the back porch of the kitchen where supplies were unloaded from trucks and we both stopped dead when we heard a *thunk*! of metal struck violently on metal to our left.

Wham! *Wham*! was coming from the room off the kitchen which housed two side-by-side walk-in coolers, one for meats, one for fruits and vegetables.

Yvonne's right hand, fingers spread, flew to her throat and lingered a moment, fingers toying with a thin gold chain from which depended no locket or charm.

"*Sonofabitch*!" cried a reedy voice within.

A look of irritation crossed Yvonne's face; she turned from me, jerked the door open and stepped in, leaving me outside on the walk: "*Donnie*! *Stop that*! *But immediately*!" she cried in a peremptory teacher's voice, and I jerked the flimsy screen door and bounded inside, ready for anything.

Donnie Redpath, angular and taut as stretched barbed wire, eyes bleary, leaned against a huge cutting block made from the bole of an immense tree—its radius was probably around two feet—weaving and embattled, the kitchen's meat cleaver dangling from one long-fingered hand.

There were gleaming raw scars on the heavy padlock securing the bolt on the meat cooler door—clearly Donnie'd been trying to break in by knocking the lock to pieces and would likely have succeeded had he not been caught in the act by his aunt.

Donnie's rheumy eyes were fixed on Yvonne, who faced him angrily, elbows akimbo, fists balled at either hip like some caricature of a school-marm. Then he focussed on me and a light seemed to go on in his eyes: "What're you lookin' at, jerk?" he croaked in a husky voice edged with threat. He reeked of beer and there was a large tear-shaped blotch of wetness on the breast of his Delta Tau Delta sweatshirt.

I smiled, calculating and estimating, then did the one thing I thought certain to infuriate him: stepped up beside Yvonne, elaborately hooded my eyes with one hand, bent at my waist, and looked him slowly up and down, then laughed, not loudly, but a sort of coarse chuckle implying I found him almost as humorous as, say, the Three Stooges. Curly, say.

He turned from both of us, lifted high the cleaver, and brought it whistling down, embedding its far end in the butcherblock a good two inches, his long-boned body supplying plenty of leverage. Yvonne stepped back with a little gasp, as though realizing for the first time this blood relative of hers was shit-faced and potentially dangerous.

When he turned I don't think he saw her anymore: everything was blocked out except me: his long-fingered hands formed substantial fists and he began to advance on me.

I didn't move as he drew back his right arm—then did when he uncorked his punch. He was off-balance and it was pitifully easy to step aside and let him hurtle past, carried forward by his roundhouse swing, which generated wind but didn't touch anything.

It further amused me that he tripped as he sailed by me

hunched over, his right fist thrust forward like an outrigger, punching through the flimsy screen door and out into the night, even as he lost his balance and fell to his knees at the threshold, stymied by the door.

Then I stepped forward, grasped him by the thick collar of his frat-rat sweatshirt with one hand, hooked my fingers beneath the belt of his chinos belt with the other, and lifted him off the floor and held him there, ready to propel him forward in a kind of horizontal frog-march-carry.

I swung Donnie back a little and set myself for a great heave that would send him crashing into the screen door and then, I hoped, carried by his own weight, out onto the pavement—when Yvonne put her hands around my shoulders from behind: "Miller, oh, Miller, please *don't*, can't you see he's *drunk*, he barely knows what he's doing . . . Miller, put him down and wait outside for a minute, *please* . . . Let me deal with this . . ."

* * *

I sat outside on the wooden bench next to the humming refrigeration apparatus for the walk-ins and massaged my face with hands. I was able to hear some of Yvonne's and Donnie's chat.

" . . . and just *what* do you think your *parents* would make of *that* little display? Breaking into family property and gratuitously *ruining* things when anything you really want is yours for the asking . . . threatening, or close to it, to split your aunt's head open with a meat cleaver? The *idea*! Donnie? *Donnie*?"

"Jus' wanned somea that roas' beef is all, Aunt Yvonne . . ."

"Well, you don't have to *smash* things to get it . . ."

This went on for two or three minutes.

Then I heard his last words on the situation: "Yes, ma'am," uttered seriously, even contritely, without a hint of mockery or sarcasm. Then, so low I barely heard it: "I'm sorry, Aunt Yvonne . . . Jeez, I din't mean to . . ."

* * *

"You didn't need to be all that *violent* with him, Miller . . ."

"Hey, that clown was dangerous, nephew or not, he had a *cleaver* . . . Chrissakes, he took a swing at me, he might've hurt *you*, even . . ."

"Oh, I know . . . but he was *drunk* . . ."

I felt a surly response, *Yes ma'am, Auntie Yvonne, Ah'm powerful sorry, I reeely am, won'tcher fergive me*? But wisely kept my trap shut—I might use humor, even sarcasm, with Yvonne, I sensed, but never mockery.

With her next breath Yvonne murmured, "Only friction could make him warm or violence make him mobile . . ."

"I don't know what you mean . . ."

"I know, I know, oh, and it's not fair of me, just another goddamn literary quote, a point of association. That's from *Miss Lonelyhearts* by the *much* underestimated Nathaniel West, also one of HG's favorite writers, incidentally. Well, Miller, I'm done, and now I'm ready to quit my school teacher persona and return to my previous one as . . . what was I? Temptress? No, in*triguer*, that's right . . ."

"That's right," I said, smiling at her. "And I reckon I'm the intrigued, that's pretty accurate . . ."

* * *

We continued to walk slowly up the winding drive past the kitchen, then veered to our right onto a two rut gravel road, and seemed to float over to the little pod of four cabins, all sharing at least two walls with an adjoining cabin.

We stepped under the cabin's overhang—it shadowed us so we were completely in the dark—and Yvonne stepped up on the punky doorstep and without hesitation pulled the screen door open. Its spring was broken and the door swung back silently. I went to pull the cord and turn on the 60-watt bulb dangling from the ceiling but Yvonne touched my forearm and handed me a candle and a pack of paper matches from one of her pockets. "We've no need for electric lights, have we?"

Yvonne didn't speak again until I'd lit the candle and tipped it to spill a few drops of festive red wax on the dresser across from the bed. I stuck the candle in the wax before it cooled.

"My, isn't this quaint and cozy and intimate . . . 'a small room, even a tiny room, but one sufficient to contain us both'—that's a line from one of my better stories, in which there's a situation, wholly imagined I might add, not entirely unlike this one . . ."

Yes, the room was tiny, no more than ten by twelve, probably, with a single bunk built against the wall, the only other items of furniture a beat-up dresser with a big oval mirror and a single fold-up auditorium chair facing the bunk—my knapsack sat on the chair, the foot of a sock lolling from its main flap like a tongue.

Yvonne plumped herself down on the spartan bunk, wriggling her shoulders in her blue-black sweater, closely examining my bed-making job—I'd done it earlier with sheets and a light blanket and a thin rayon spread that felt slick as nylon ('as panties,' remarked an unsteady voice in the back of my head). I noticed for the first time that it was royal blue onto which lighter blue ship's-wheels had been embroidered.

Suddenly I felt a little pissed, wondered if I were being condescended to, spoken at rather than to in a tone that didn't tell you what was what: and so did what Doc Knowles would surely have advised ("Brazen it out!"), sat down next to Yvonne, put an arm around her shoulders, turned her face toward mine with my other hand, and kissed her full on the mouth and for real.

For only a moment was Yvonne lax in my arms, then she put her arms around me and drew me deeper into the kiss I'd begun, continuing it, elongating it and, it seemed, time itself until, with my eyes shut tight, I found myself travelling somewhere almost entirely new.

When we broke off the kiss for air, Yvonne murmured, "Whoever said I was supposed to be a plaster saint anyhow?"

"Certainly not me."

"You're getting rather a smart mouth for someone who projects such an un-self-assuming persona . . . and yes, and I do like your hands on my neck and ears like that . . ."

What followed was memorable for its smoothness and ease, everything as natural as leaves dropping from maples in autumn: no awkward jerking or pulling, just a slow gentle tugging and a slow unwrapping and revelation of ourselves, our hands performing dexterously in the shedding of her shorts and sweater (beneath which she wore nothing) and my sweatshirt and trunks until we found ourselves mouth to mouth, breath to breath, chest to chest, her nipples hardening, our small groans and sighs bleeding together like colors in an oil slick. We shifted slowly and without urgency from vertical to horizontal, then wriggled until we lay sideways, facing each other on the narrow bunk. Before I could touch I was touched; before fondle, fondled: that a woman might initiate these things astonished and dazzled me.

The wet blossom of her pussy with its textures of satin and fur, with its velvet channel moistening itself beneath my fingers, sent all words skeltering from my head, just as well for they certainly weren't needed: Yvonne was able to suggest what she'd like done and how I might please her through a whole series of intricate little proddings, pressings and tuggings whose dictates I followed gladly until at last she lay beneath me and we writhed against each other, kissing, tongues buried in one another's mouths until we broke for air, then my head dipped like a drinking bird's to her budded nipples, exploring with my tongue the pebbly aureoles and incredible softness of the surrounding breasts. When I entered her, it occurred to me for the first time in my life that making love was the correct term for what we were about.

"God, Yvonne, I . . ."

"Miller . . . my dear . . . whew . . ."

"Yvonne . . ."

"Could you just slow down for a minute, my dear . . ."

""Like this . . ."

"Yes. Now stop . . . that's right, I . . . Miller, lift up and come out of me just for now . . ."

"Okay . . ."

"Yes . . . now . . . *there*!" Fingers wet from our mutual juices, Yvonne drew my cock upward, then downward, almost making me faint, each time on the upstroke stopping at the top of her pussy and rubbing me around into her, then lowering and at her opening just letting me in a bit, then continuing the pattern of circular movements: I was going to come but was powerless; I felt her breath, heard her passionate but unintelligible murmuring in my ear; then she pushed me forcefully into her and lifted against me, nails digging into my back, crying out "*God*! *God*!" And I fainted forward into a red haze of what could only have been ecstasy.

For long moments neither of us moved save that I shuddered every time her vaginal muscles tightened.

"Well, what do you think?" Yvonne asked as scattered parts of myself seemed to be reassembling themselves. Moments or minutes had passed, which seemed unimportant.

"About what?"

"Oh, you're a great kidder, aren't you? Well, I approve. Somewhere, I think it's in 'Fate,' Emerson says 'We must see the world is rough and surly, and will not mind drowning a man or a woman' . . . who knows, maybe humor and sex are all we really have against the . . . absurdity of things. But of course I was referring to *us*. Our new estate, so to speak . . ."

"New estate? . . ."

"Yes: for we're *lovers* now. Becoming lovers is an infinitely hopeful and optimistic act, Miller, made all the more precious because we're always aware of 'Time's wing'ed chariot hurrying near.' Isn't lovers a lovely word? Doesn't it have almost a kind of, oh, in*can*tatory quality: Lovers. You see? The way the word comes from . . . well, the way it moves up through you and slides off your tongue like cool liquid silver? You're my lover. I'm your lover. We're lovers, at least for now—now you try it . . ."

"Lovers," I croaked, "You're my lover and I love you—"

"—*No*! Oh, *no*, silly, you're not supposed to go *that* far . . ."

"Lovers," I said slowly, my face suffused with blood, glad the candle shed no more light than it did. "Lovers."

"That's more like it, my dear, two syllables without much of an interval . . . and in some way in spite of the transiency of all things, we'll always be that, even in six thousand million years or so when the sun runs out of hydrogen and swells up and engulfs the planets, *still* some part of us that was lovers will still be there embodied in a dead but gleaming White Dwarf hanging in the sky . . . once we're lovers, we will never not be lovers in a sense. God! Think of Abélard and Héloïse side-by-side in the Père Lachaise in Paris . . ."

I fell asleep with Yvonne pressed against me, her breath soft on my ears and neck.

Later I awoke and found her sitting on the bunk beside me, naked, looking down on me, smiling, hand lightly encircling my cock. "Gather ye rosebuds while ye may," she murmured.

"'Old time is still a-flying,'" I answered. "'And this same flower that smiles today, Tomorrow will be dying' . . ."

And to think fellow students at the Ermine Falls School had mocked me for spending many study hall hours memorizing parts of Elizabethan poems that caught my fancy. Maybe I had been prescient without knowing it. Last summer Doc Knowles lent me his *Norton Anthology of English Literature, Volume 1*, and his syllabus for British Lit 1, and by now I'd done virtually all the readings. I seemed to have a knack for recalling passages from poems, though seldom the entire work.

Yvonne lay down beside me again and as we touched from noses to toes, she whispered, "Here's another quote for you: 'Ripeness is all.'"

Larry's Birthday

June 20, 1949

Mrs. Gracious Carstairs, principal of the Ermine Falls School, came out to the shop on a Thursday in June after school'd been out for about two weeks and talked to Turner, and Turner sent Rex, who was working in the back cleaning up and degreasing several bell housings, up to the house to get me.

When I got down to the shop in jeans and T-shirt—I didn't even bother with shoes—my heart sank, though I couldn't remember having done anything recently that anyone would consider too dreadful.

I felt a little better when I saw Turner's bemused smile as he motioned me over to where he and Mrs. Carstairs stood by the desk that held his adding machine and his thick car parts catalogues and accounting ledgers.

"Go right ahead and speak to him, Mrs. Carstairs . . ."

Gracious Carstairs looked warmly at me. We were eye-to-eye so she was about five-three. She was vigorous and stocky, with platinum hair with a bluish tinge, and a ready smile; I'd never seen her other than perky, talkative and energetic and had always liked her. Her kid Larry was okay too, though he was kind of a loner—as I suppose an only child town kid with a teacher for a mother pretty much has to be. I'd never had much to do with Larry except when we played softball, at which he was pretty good: fast and wiry, solid at bat and a decent infielder.

"Miller, I know you and Larry aren't especially close, but I would certainly take it as a personal favor if you'd come to a little birthday celebration for his ninth birthday this Sunday evening . . . I, well, Clayton Knowles is coming over and his younger brother Tucker is coming as well, oh, and also Larry's friend from Vulcan, Welles Stringer. So you and Tucker'll be third graders and the others will be fourth graders . . ."

I looked to Turner but he wouldn't give away anything in his look to tell me what I ought to do. So I said, "Sure, that's real nice of you, Missus Carstairs . . ." (Somewhere in the back of my head I was a little pissed I'd got into a position where I couldn't say no.)

"Why don't you come around 6:00 or just a little after, and we'll have some cake and ice cream. And I *promise* I won't hang around all the time and make you uncomfortable, this is for Larry, not me, after all . . ." And she made a funny kind of tittering giggle expressing a little embarrassment and a lot of confidence. Then she said it wasn't necessary to bring a gift, though we all three knew it was.

* * *

"It's likely a good thing you're going," Turner told me at supper, "she's a real nice woman and her kid looks fine too, but he's a shy one. Once I heard Gracious tell somebody maybe the reason Larry didn't talk much was because he couldn't get a word in edgewise, and then she give that laugh of hers . . ."

"You could've come up with something you needed me for," I said. "Chores of some kind?"

"Yes, but it would've sounded like a lie because it would've been a lie . . . 'sides, since you live in an all-male household, now you can check out the reverse and see what you make of it—Ermine Falls's a town, after all, not just a four corners . . ." I suddenly understood his amused look.

I hadn't thought of that. Anyway, I'd always wanted to look around inside the Carstairs house. And since there was no graceful way to get out of this, there was no point in pissing and moaning.

* * *

A little before 6:00 on Sunday, Turner picked up Doc and Tucker down the road and we all rode into town scrunched into his pickup. Instead of pulling into the Carstairs' drive, he let us off by the road—I suspected he wasn't too keen about getting caught in a chat for however long Mrs. Carstairs might like.

Just as Turner was ready to drive off, Welles Stringer's mother Mildred pulled up in her old Plymouth and dropped Welles off. Turner gave Mildred, like Gracious Carstairs a widow in her forties, a wave and a smile and pulled away without a backward glance. I thought: Here's these two nice widows just about Turner's age, and he gets along nice with them and can talk pretty damn smooth when he wants to . . . wonder why he never lets things go any further, wonder if he might ever go a-courting again—and was grateful it didn't seem likely. Turner and Rex and I were doing just fine now and needed no additions to our household, especially a perky woman who talked a lot and who probably had plenty of ideas about how Rex and I ought to be raised. Larry by himself would probably have been all right. That he wasn't much of a talker was fine with me.

By now Doc and Tucker and I, carrying our presents in our hands, were hollering hello to Welles Stringer, round-headed and kind of pudgy, as we all made for the front door, which Gracious Carstairs swung back before I could rap the big brass knocker with CARSTAIRS on it, disappointing me a little—I'd wanted to hear what the knocker sounded like. As we were ushered in, she relieved each of us of our presents with little exclamations—"Oh, how lovely . . . what pretty paper!"—and put them on a buffet in the living room.

The Carstairs house was a clean, lemon-smelling one-story frame house ("Our bungalow," Mrs. Carstairs called it) mostly given over to a big dining room and living room. There were three small bedrooms. Two huge, mostly-blue oriental carpets covered most of the living room and dining room floors and in the living room was a brick fireplace and various kinds of pictures on the walls, watercolors mostly of game birds like ducks and pheasants and geese. The fireplace's mantel was cluttered with photographs, many of them of Larry at a young age, and on either end were two big beer steins with conical lids you could press back with a thumb. But the dining room table made everything else go sort of pale.

Mrs. Carstairs saw me looking in at it from the living room and came up to me and took me by the elbow and pulled me away from the others over to it. Five places were set on a blazing white tablecloth with deep creases, as if it'd recently come out of storage. There were large linen napkins rolled and placed in silver rings. But most startling were the dishes we were going to eat on: each had a different scene from London and looked very old. The places were set with pearl-handled silver knives and forks and spoons and there were big cut glass goblets with designs cut on their sides. A big bottle of Vernor's Ginger Ale sat in a small, shiny bucket of ice. I noticed there was nothing set at the horse-hair-bottomed head-of-household chair that had been Gracious' husband's. Delbert Carstairs had been killed on D-Day, Turner told me.

"Those are my 'Cries of London' plates, Miller, and these mother-of-pearl-handled implements were given to me by my mother-in-law years ago and came from Marshal Fields in Chicago. My mother gave me my cut glass—I have a lot more. Isn't it pretty? Oh. Well, I did promise not to monopolize things, didn't I? I'll absent myself from felicity a while, now, and let you boys socialize, and within half an hour or so I'll serve you some cake and ice cream and then make another timely exit . . ."

She sped off to inform the others while I gazed at the place setting before me: it was mine because there was a little name card in fancy script on the plate. Beside the silverware was a cylindrical party favor with a string you pulled at one end.

Larry had emerged from somewhere, looking uncomfortable, and was saying something to Welles while Tucker and Doc listened.

* * *

Back in the living room with Gracious off in her bedroom we all sat around at first, Welles and Larry on the sofa, Tucker on the over-stuffed chair, Doc and I on the matching wing chairs before the fireplace. Silence descended on us and nobody said anything. Larry, looking bewildered, sat chewing on his lower lip, eyes darting from one guest to the other, and I suddenly understood that this shindig had been entirely his mother's operation and he was embarrassed.

Finally, I got up and went over to the opposite side of the room that was covered with two huge bookcases—they must have had a couple of hundred books, more than I'd ever seen outside of the Vulcan library.

When I turned from my study of titles, none of which I recognized, save a few Thorton Burgess books like those that I learned to read with, I saw Welles and Tucker and Doc had arisen and gone to stand before a blushing Larry as he stood at the buffet, unwrapping each gift, all wrapped more or less alike in leftover Christmas paper and tied with ribbon.

From Doc, a magnifying glass. "Gee, thanks, Doc," Larry said. "This is just great. I like to spend a lot of time watching ant hills and doodle-bug holes, and this's just the thing . . ."

"You can fry the bastards too, if you want to focus the sun's beam on'em," Tucker said, eyeing his gift as Larry unwrapped it: not much mystery there, it was round and could have been identified as a softball from ten paces. It was a nice one, slightly used. "Gee, thanks Tucker . . ." Larry was looking more embarrassed each time he opened a present. Once in Guilder's, I heard someone say to Gracious, "Gosh, Larry's a quiet kid, isn't he?" "Yes," she'd answered quickly, "and he's just the *best* boy, he can go off and be alone and amuse himself for hours on end without any supervision . . ."

Welles Stringer's was something thin and square. Larry opened it to find a mirror, shiny on one side and black on the other. It had a hole in one corner through which a stout khaki nylon cord passed. Immediately Welles was at Larry's side, explaining it: "Y'see, this is a army surplus signal mirror, Larry, see here on the back where it's all black and you look through this clear little X here and you use that to aim your beam of sunlight, you can flash this son-of-a-bitch up to thirty miles away . . . they used 'em in the Signal Corps in the war . . . s'posed to be unbreakable too . . ."

Peering through it, Larry smiled deeply, entranced. "Shit," he said, "let's go out and try it out before the sun's all the way down . . ."

"Here, Larry . . ." I picked up my foot-long package, eager to get my part over. My package's contents were not much harder to guess than Tucker's softball. But when Larry opened it he smiled and it looked like real interest lighting his eyes: I'd given him two *Classic Illustrated* comics of two Jack London books, *White Fang* and *The Call of the Wild* I'd found in the glove compartment of a wrecked Ford station wagon Turner'd brought home from auction on our flatbed truck a few weeks ago. They were almost new and I'd hated to part with them.

* * *

We were all in the backyard fifteen minutes later on our knees facing west, taking turns looking through the signal mirror at the lowering sun and trying to target the bloody beams we created at fenceposts and trees, when Gracious Carstairs opened the front door and called, "Come on in, boys, quickly, before the ice cream melts! Your ginger ale's *perfectly* chilled by now, and I'm eager to pour!"

* * *

"So how'd it go, "Turner asked after we'd dropped Doc and Tucker off and were alone in the pickup. "Have a good time? Maybe now you figure a lady's influence is a necessity for a well-rounded household?"

"I dunno, Pa . . . it was kinda strange. The plates. Cries of London. And silver with pearl handles. I'd be afraid to live where everything was some kind of special deal and wasn't just plain stuff to eat on or use. Lottsa books and these big pretty rugs Mrs. Carstairs called Persian, and a nice brick fireplace."

For some reason I recalled the cylindrical party favors where you pulled a cord and it went *pop*! and there was a little bit of cap-pistol smoke in the air and then you could pull out a folded party hat. For some reason none of us touched them, maybe thinking they were kid stuff. For some reason I thought of the party hats of tight-folded flimsy and colorful tissue paper still compressed within the favors. I wondered if Gracious had collected them after we'd gone and put them away for some future use.

"Yeah?" Turner was waiting for more.

"Yeah. I was almost afraid to drink from any cut glass stuff, or really press my fork through the cake for fear of scratching one of those Cries of London plates . . ."

The one I'd eaten from had shown a young woman in a long, old-fashioned dress with a boy and a girl of ten or so next to her and a dog sniffing her skirt. The woman had a basket of flowers and to the left of the scroll that said "Cries of London" the legend in English read "Two Bunches a Penny Primroses." Gracious had taken great pleasure in pointing out that to the right of the scroll was the same thing in French. The background had been a building against which a huddled gray figure buried its face in its hands. "Mrs. Carstairs told me the designs on her wine goblets were 'incised' by special olden-time engravers . . . the handles of the silverware were 'mother of pearl' . . ."

"Have wine in'em, did they?"

"Nah—ginger ale. Vernor's."

"You don't say. How'd Larry like his Classics comics?"

"He did, he's a real reader, likes all kinds of comics . . . say, they got a ton of books in that house and Mrs. Carstairs said she'd lend me any I wanted to read."

"Good thing we got the Vulcan Library."

"Why do you say that?"

"Well, you don't have to worry so much about whether you might get a fingerprint on'em, and you don't need to take any quizzes over what you read . . . not that that's a bad thing . . ."

"Yeah, I see what you mean . . . say, Larry really liked this army surplus signal mirror Welles Stringer gave him, something he claimed they used in the Signal Corps . . . I saw Larry's room, he's got tons and tons of comics but he seemed real glad to get the Classics . . ."

"Yeah. Well, being an only child I reckon he's a lucky kid in some ways," Turner said slowly, "and in some ways maybe he's not so lucky . . ."

My father looked directly into my eyes, and his gaze was somber. "I reckon the same could be said for you and Rex," he said.

Chapter Five

When I awakened, Yvonne was close but not touching, propped up on one elbow, looking at me, dark eyes lustrous in the faint starshine permitted by cheesecloth curtains over the cabin's single window. "Hiya," she said.

"Hiya yourself."

"I'm glad you're awake. I was thinking I should get up and get dressed and go, but I still had some things I wanted to explain to you . . ."

"Sure."

"It has to do with how we got together, you and I, and about Harrison, too, and how things got to be sort of . . . as they are, and how Chekhov fits into the equation. How would you like a little quiz? Can you remember the last thing I quoted you last night?"

"'Ripeness is all'?"

"Yes. This is asking too much, but do you happen to know where it comes from? It doesn't matter, I was just curious . . ."

"Edgar says it in *King Lear* . . ."

"My lover, the autodidact."

"So go on, tell me whatever it is . . ."

"I will, though I'm afraid parts may be boring, but I don't have time to edit out the bad lines like I'd do if I were revising a story . . . anyhow, Harrison— 'HG' as his dwindling numbers of friends and colleagues call him—started as a pure academic, Miller, and he was very conventional so far as everyone knew. He'd dabbled with creative writing in undergrad, but who hadn't. And he wrote a *very* good dissertation on Harold Frederic's late nineteenth century novel *The Damnation of Theron Ware*. Later on, he chopped it up and got two articles, one appeared in the PMLA, the other in *American Literature*. *Very* quality publications, upper tier as they say, for someone who was just an assistant professor—that's just the second rung up on the academic ladder,

Miller, so things looked auspicious. Because of the publications, he was boosted to associate professor, and he was on a tenure track, but to get tenure, you see, and to get up to full professor, he had to come up with some more first tier scholarly publications. Maybe it helps to know that what drew Harrison to me originally was not my good looks"—Yvonne lifted and shook her head and batted her eyes in parody of coquettishness—"nor my fabulously lush body, but the fact that I wrote short stories, not that he cared much about the stories themselves. As an undergrad I edited the college litmag and had a few stories in other college litmags. Even after I graduated and right up to the present moment I keep writing short stories—it's a fascinating and tremendously demanding form. I've probably little hope of getting my best ones collected in a book—Lord, I've only published seven in over eight years. But I seem to need to do it and I like having something that totally fascinates and preoccupies me when I'm doing it. A little like us together, you might say . . .

"But it was otherwise with Harrison. His ambition became monomaniacal, like Ahab pursuing the white whale: he'd write a novel and get it published, and he deliberately made all his decisions around the novel. He figured he had two choices: the first was to keep single and on his own and live cheaply and raggedly and put everything he had into the novel, and if necessary lie, cheat and steal to get the work done, as Faulkner advised in his *Paris Review* interview. Or, second, he could play it foxily, live within the establishment, be a mild-mannered prof by day, conventional and responsible and dull, and then go home at night and blaze away at the novel. 'Live like a bourgeois, think like a demigod,' as Flaubert put it. And as you can see, he chose the latter option and asked me to marry him. And so, in 1953, I became a part of his plan. I had teaching credentials and a modest trust fund and also I could help him type and edit his manuscripts—he even envisioned me typing all his final drafts. You see, I was a foot-soldier in his war where the enemy was something called the 'Establishment,' the 'System,' that Harrison always felt was *totally* inimical to him . . . I told him paranoiacs were made, not born, ho ho, but that wasn't amusing to him, *no*, besides, he never put much stock in *my* conclusions . . ."

I was beginning to find this a little tedious, not because her story was necessarily uninteresting, but because it had nothing to do with her and me and our affair or whatever it was that we were caught up in, and already I wanted her again, deep down, now that I knew what she contained, and I wondered if I caressed her now if she'd want me or repel me. So perhaps, a little like "Harrison Goode versus the System" I took the middle path of concealing my yearnings (for the moment): "So tell me what the novel was about and how his, uh, quest turned out . . ." And ran my hand lightly but firmly along the lovely flare from midsection to hips and was gratified that my caress gave her voice a little catch when she started to speak again, and that she inclined—or seemed to incline—her body toward me a bit.

"Well, he started pretty strongly: *Clumsy Partners* was half-finished before the semester break, a little under two hundred pages double-spaced, and HG planned to pay attention to his classes and the essay on Harold Frederic he was writing that when published would punch his academic ticket. He'd complete the second half of the novel when summer came and he could give it everything he had . . ."

"What was the story about?" I asked, starting to feel a little drowsy beneath my accruing desire.

"Write about what you know, isn't that what they say? Well, *Clumsy Partners* was about a young would-be academic at a straight-laced state university in the Midwest who was a newlywed, had a drinking problem, and was starting his first year of full-time teaching and marriage as he worked on his dissertation on Frederic's *The Damnation of Theron Ware* . . . and guess what comes along to complicate things? Why, his bride, Honoria (I suspect he cribbed the name from Fitzgerald's 'Babylon Revisited'), who bears a passing resemblance to, guess who? Well, I hate to tell you this, Miller, but alas poor Honoria, she dies of a nasty old aortic aneurysm, rare but not unheard of in an otherwise healthy young woman—he made her dark blond, by the way—subtle, eh? As for the young husband, now widower, Kevin LeBlanc, the narrator, what happens to *him*? Easy—he stays half-drunk for days, weeks, months, can't bear to work on his thesis, turns up for most of his classes but is only marginally there, his drinking escalates and we can see he's inching ineluctably toward what's commonly known as the brink. Emerson said that 'for every seeing soul there are but two absorbing facts,—I and the Abyss,' and God knows it was so for Harrison's protagonist. At any rate, to make it short, Miller, one fine day in April he drives up north to the summer resort where he and Honoria met and courted. So off he goes, swilling Old Grand-Dad and chasing it with beer as he tools north in his beat-up VW . . . of course he's blotto by the time he gets to where he's going, which is, guess where?"

She paused, my cue to answer or comment. No doubt she was checking to see if I were paying attention because I had been tracing and re-tracing the curve of her hip with my index finger. "Sure. The Champs, under another name."

"Yes. Good. As you've perceived, he was writing what they call a *roman à clef*. Yes. Well, Kevin's there to drink and reminisce at good old Kingsblood. Yes, Kingsblood is the resort's name, and of course it bears more than a passing resemblance to this place. I won't go into the complications, some of which appear in flashbacks, but finally at a sodden moment near the end he decides that like the heroine of Kate Chopin's *The Awakening* he'll strip off his clothes and swim out into the drink until he tires to the point that he can't make it back. So as you and I did earlier this evening, Miller, he leaps naked into the cold water of Lake Aden and commences to stroke toward the lake's center, about a mile out (Kevin-Harrison was always a pretty good swimmer). He quickly tires, however, and it would seem that the end of our misunderstood and harassed-by-life hero, Kevin LeBlanc . . . but *wait*: he gets a sudden turn of heart or mind, or maybe just fear, but he tells himself what a sad testament to his lovely late wife his suicide'd be, so he turns around and starts swimming back to shore. He's drunk, cold, tired—will he have the wherewithal to make it back? Does he really want to? He looks off into the murk and a light comes on in the boathouse at Kingsblood . . . he relaxes, feels the golden light pulling him home . . . and he's happy for the first time in his life . . .

"There the book ends. Is it a vision, that light? Or is it real as the green light at the end of the Buchanan's dock that so bewitched Gatsby? Who knows? Does he survive his dip? Who knows? The end."

I'd absorbed the details of *Clumsy Partners* but my attention was now mostly on Yvonne's hips, and belly and thighs, separated from me by no more than half a foot; as much from Yvonne's tone as from her information, I was beginning to see Harrison as a kind of upper-crust version of Odell Knowles, Doc's hapless father: he who certainly put his shoulder to the wheel with a will—but his feet seemed planted on soft slippery clay that gave no solid purchase as he was pushed further into the past.

Yvonne startled me by saying: "Do you know the precise moment when I decided it might be possible for us to be lovers, Miller?"

"Uh, no . . ."

"Then I'll tell you, it was when I came into the kitchen this evening and saw your copy of *The Viking Portable Chekhov* on the serving counter. Anyone who works in the story form regards Chekhov as the greatest short story writer of all. And now I'm just dying to know, which of his stories do you like best?"

"Uh, 'Gooseberries' . . ." That story and "The Darling" and "Misery" and "About Love" were the only ones I'd thus far read. Now that I thought about it, I probably liked "Misery," the shortest, best: the end made you feel as if you'd been jabbed simultaneously in the heart and eye with a needle.

"I love that one, too—and it's a kind of companion piece to my all-time favorite, 'The Lady with the Pet Dog.' Anyway, I saw the book there and your bookmark in it, and it occurred to me there probably wasn't another young man in all of Skeegemog County—or Grand Traverse, for that matter—who at that moment was reading Chekhov. And that it was you, whom I very much liked, made it all the better. Anyway, Miller, tonight was the end of three years of celibacy—I thought once I was up to the challenge but tonight proved I wasn't. I don't mean like you're an *experiment* or something, far, oh, far, far from it. But aren't we lucky? Self-gratification only goes so far, I mean we're human, we've a *need* to be touched and held and kissed and fondled and made love to, it's a necessary connection to the world of others. I believe sex is the greatest celebration of existence there is, and I'm just no longer up to living a life of such deprivation. Of course, there's *always* some selfishness involved with sex, but it wouldn't be any good if there weren't. You're supposed to kiss me now. And touch me and all the rest," and before I could move she was in my arms again, warm and breathy, lightly sweating and clearly wanting me every bit as much as I wanted her. "But now let's sort of touch and just lie here and be affectionate and sort of simmer for a while . . . here, darling, put your hand here and hold it like this and don't move too awful much and when the time's right, we'll make love again—that is, if you'd like to . . ."

"There, like that?"

"Yes . . . here, let me hold you like this . . ."

And so I told her what I knew she wanted to hear: "Tell me the rest. About you and Harrison and his novel."

* * *

"So the second semester—the second semester of our married life too, I might add—HG got so frazzled he finally let the big essay on Harold Frederic go by the boards, and at night he worked compulsively, almost savagely, on the novel. Dutiful wife that I was, I typed and helped edit it, sort of, though any real expertise I had was in short forms . . ."

"Did he think of you as competition?"

"A very good question—no, that was one noteworthy deliverance. He understood the truth, that I only worked on small canvases, and had no ambition beyond just wanting to get down what I could. God! A piece in a literary magazine once a year or so and my cup runneth over. But to be brief, I typed the manuscript of his novel, and he found a publisher, Bayard Duke, who'd once been executive editor with Viking and who'd now started Duke Publications, a small commercial publisher who distributed through Dutton. HG was in heaven. He worked the script over with me, with Duke, and then it was copyedited and sent back to him; he went over it and sent it back. Then, nothing. For weeks. Duke's phone was disconnected. HG finally discovered Duke had had a stroke and was in the hospital, Duke Publications was finished, *kaput*. Just as HG had finished lying to his department head about the delay in publication of his novel, the copy-edited manuscript was sent back—not to our home address but to Harrison at school. It was sent to him fourth class, like, as he put it while he still retained at least a tittle of humor, 'a god-damned Sears and Roebuck catalogue.' It was the beginning of the end. I'll never forget how Harrison looked at home that night, sitting there on our comfortable green sofa, the big mailing envelope thrown on the floor, and on his knees the edited and copy-edited manuscript. I was outraged, I remember thinking, 'They can't do this! It's been edited! Copy-edited! There, you see those red copy-editor's marks on the pages? Those marks are for the *typesetter*, it's ready to be made into a book! He has a *contract*, you bastards!' I threw myself across HG's lap—I could feel the ugly manuscript pushing up at me—and wept while he sat there with a blank look on his face . . . I think he started dying a little faster at that moment . . .

"Later, he tried other publishers and agents, and every now and then he'd come close, or the sympathetic rejection letters he got made it sound that way, who knows what's really going on with the New York City 'litbiz,' as Harrison used to call it. And after a time, everything got thin—the script went out fewer times, there were fewer letters of declination from editors and agents, his correspondence—he used to write to other people he'd met in grad school who were writing—thinned, disappeared, the manuscript was put away or destroyed—who knows, I haven't seen it in three years, and then came the alienation whose sort of terminal throes you got here in time to at least partially witness. It continues to this day, with nothing fun or pleasant or bracing or cheering in the offing, nothing but doom and gloom and stasis and drink, drink, drink . . . maybe Harrison can't get his novel published like his hero Malcolm Lowry but he sure can drink like him . . . or like Lowry did until he washed down a bunch of sleeping pills with a quart of gin and fell through what Faulkner called 'the wall of oblivion.' One fortunate aspect was that, due to our respective literary aspirations, neither of us wanted children and soon after we were married I got a tubal ligation—which is handy now, isn't it, since we don't have to deal with icky condoms or foams or diaphragms or any other clunky things, there's nothing needed between us but *us*, not that I expect any of that to really be a concern of *yours* . . .

"Oh, and you know the biggest irony—*Clumsy Partners* wasn't a bad novel, at least in my humble opinion, not a knockout, but sound and competently written, and oh, Miller, yes, that feels nice, maybe we should just forget about the god-damned book that was almost a book for a while, shall we? . . ."

In answer, I brought my dampened fingers up and caressed her nipples, then licked off the exquisite sheen, savoring the scent, not unknown but never really enjoyed before this night, causing her to shudder with each swipe of my tongue, then her cool fingers lightly touched my temples and exerted just enough pressure to suggest I move downward rather than upward . . . as I did, licking away a curving line of silver sweat beneath her breasts, then down her rib cage until I was kissing and licking her belly-button, likewise eliciting shudders, then down into her lovely pussy-fragrant bush, burrowing a bit with my nose until I touched silken skin and wetness and Yvonne shuddered and groaned and lifted herself up against me and I lost myself in this new and fantastic series of sensations all happening at once, taste, touch, smell, and let her, by pressing my temples, suggest to me where I might go to thrill her most, holding me in place when she found some particularly responsive spot; and underneath was a nubbin of joy at having her take the initiative and move us to our mutual delight: now she was pulling me up and over her, wanting me inside her as much as I yearned to be there and then we were both thrusting and gasping and I had no idea where she began and I left off and she cried out and looped an arm around my neck and crushed me to her for a few seconds, then relaxed as I groaned in my own ecstasy and we drowned into each other, then lay quiescent, skin to skin, pulse to pulse, lip to lip, until I began to swell and she stirred in response and desire sprang up again like a sudden breeze off the lake.

As we made love, this time in an almost leisurely way, as if we both had infinite time and had determined to never be rushed, she murmured half to herself but in my ear, "I don't know, but I guess I really think now it was a mediocre novel . . . of course that's only an opinion . . ."

I licked Yvonne's shoulder, nibbled her ear, and urgency returned. Afterwards, lassitude, during which I was aware of her getting out of bed and dressing but I kept my eyes closed even through the light kiss on my cheek and the sound of the springless screen door scraping shut.

* * *

Shortly thereafter the same screen door was jerked back so hard it slammed against the side of the cabin.

I opened my eyes just as the dangling overhead bulb was jerked on and saw Rex standing there unsteadily, peering down at me, shit-faced, grinning slackly, his face drained of blood, smelling of beer.

"Hey, ole Miller, how's she going, there, pardner? . . ."

"Okay, I guess . . . Jesus, you look like something the cat dragged in . . ."

"Yeah . . . got a li'l fucked up playing Thumper, me'n muh frens . . . whatta stupid fucking game, you know it?"

"Yeah, you beat on the floor with your fists and everybody's got a sign and when somebody looks at you and makes your sign, you gotta quick go to somebody else and make his sign until somebody fucks up and has to chug a shot or a beer, right?"

"Yeah . . . kinda . . ."

He fell to his knees on the braided rug on the floor. "Y'care f'I stay here? I'm too tirea go home . . ."

By the time I said "Sure," he was curled up like a grub on the rug, beginning to snore.

As Rex slept on, I tried to sleep, but kept waking; and every time I woke I had a boner and brought the fingers of my left hand to my face to gather in again the scent of Yvonne's pussy. Finally, around 2:00 I went over to the door and stood there naked, enjoying the chill on my limbs, looking out into the dark; never had I been so aware of my cock hanging at rest between my thighs, half-swollen, too, because I could not keep my just-departed lover from continuously occupying certain parts of me. I turned quickly, pulled on my jeans, turned on the 40-watt reading light affixed to the wall just above the bed, and set the pillow up as a cushion against my back. As Rex snored raggedly on, almost obscured by my bunk's blanket I'd thrown over him, I picked up *The Viking Portable Chekhov*, got into bed, and turned to "The Lady with the Pet Dog."

I read it quickly straight through, marveling, then read it again, carefully: it was every bit as good as Yvonne had claimed; maybe even better.

Moon and Ruth Ann

June 1958

. . . I am at the Champs a little before 5:00 on the morning of Clover LaBaugh's wedding day and I dream-drowse neither fully submerged and drifting nor really awake, attuned to nothing save what occasionally inserts itself suddenly like a sharp birdcall and I think "*Lover*! *Lover*! *Lover*!" as Yvonne calls me. I like its new and lilting sound and wonder if I may already have been a lover of sorts this past summer with the girl I'd always yearned for, Ruth Ann Perkins. There was an almost audible collision when fantasy met reality and proved to me all over again they were different, but linked. But that reality which came out of fantasy was maybe the best, and maybe it was partly her smallness and the way she was so finely made and was a good three inches shorter than me. We met at the last Friday free show in August and shared the wool army blanket I'd brought as we semi-watched the first quarter of *The Petrified Forest* with our townspeople and a sprinkling of visitors from nearby towns like Vulcan and Skeegemog, keeping in the shadows cast by that fish shanty on stilts the projection booth, then slipping away into a night where the bright quarter moon and glittering stars gave everything a velvety look.

(She: small, swift, lithe, supple, sinuous, well-muscled, skin like clover honey, hair oakey, wren-perky—)

Ruth Ann was deathly afraid of being seen and reported upon by someone (she was supposed to be at a friend's house making fudge) for her parents were strict and stern and what the town called "holy rollers"—members of the By-Way Gospel Tabernacle just out of town whose adult members, perhaps forty strong, had in years past come down to the west side of the projectionist's booth on Friday show nights and sung hymns as Krazy Kat and then Laurel and Hardy warmed up the audience for the main feature: *Rock of Ages*, they sang as Stan babbled and Oliver expostulated, "This is another fine mess you've gotten me into!": *Cleft for me; let me hide myself in thee*. Once she told me her father had a razor strop to mete out punishment such as for what we were up to tonight over behind the home team dugout by the clay diamond behind the Ermine Falls School where we put my harsh, wool khaki blanket down and kissed and kissed until our lips were sore and we were like kittens in a litter not knowing where one left off and others began: and I managed to slow myself down wondering: should we really do this? but then she was touching me as I was touching her and we were both soon wriggling out of our jeans and shirts until both of us were trembling in the sultry air naked except for our white socks which blazed in the moonlight and starshine, her little anklets she'd worn in her tennis shoes and my wool athletic socks and having our socks on I think made us feel even more naked and we didn't need the slightest instruction nor did we commit a single ungraceful act, not even my getting the Trojan from my jeans' watch pocket and ripping the foil off and getting it on while she caressed my back and then I inserted myself a little way and was stopped as if by a rubber plug and Ruth Ann groaned in a mixture of frustration and desire and embarrassment . . . every time I moved a millimeter she flinched until I ceased to move and we rested locked together . . . until somewhere some generous thing began to give way and bit by bit I went slowly forward into her both of us gasping at this revelation and she was giggling and weeping and hiccuping and moving against me and once when I came up from kissing her I felt tears on her face and then I came with such force I felt it even in my clenching toes and caught breath and the roots of my hair: *Eeee*! *Eeee*! she went, clenching my neck so tightly in her strong little arms I could hardly breathe—

It had been on the tip of my tongue to tell her that I loved her, but I recalled Rex's advice, knew Turner'd agree, forced myself to keep my trap shut and murmured some endearments about her hair her eyes her nose her ears her skin her breasts her breasts her breasts with their wonderfully womanly nipples atop the small hard mounds. And I wanted to compliment her too on her arms elbows and of course her inner thighs: "God," I said, not knowing what else to say. But I knew I had to say something so I said, "You're lovely . . ."

And Ruth Ann said, "I love you too . . ." And my heart contracted, then fell. I said "You're lovely" again instead of what she wanted me to say.

We clung together and listened to the ghostly cry deep in the swampy woods behind us of a whippoorwill.

That night at home when I was naked and immersed in the tub I pulled back my foreskin to give my cock a good wash and discovered three of Ruth Ann's tightly coiled golden pubic hairs and I got a blue-steeler in about three seconds and wished I'd told her I loved her even if I didn't.

Chapter Six

I woke easily at 5:30, grateful to be alive if only so I might make love to Yvonne again: far from fatigued, I felt energized, alert, powerful, all senses acute. Despite my nocturnal expenditures the engines of sex still rode me with rowelled spurs.

I was still dazzled from last night's surfeits, and now wanted . . . what? Easy. More. And after that, more. To be with my lover again and again and again. I sprang naked from bed into the chill dark morning air, ready for anything, feeling older and smarter than when I'd arrived. Clearly it was time for another freezing swim.

I was careful not to step on the slumbering Rex.

* * *

I was a little smarter on this swim, and pulled a large pair of mottled oyster-colored sweatpants I'd found in the laundry over my trunks; then I pulled on my hooded sweatshirt.

I laughed as I skipped toward the waterfront, twirling a chlorine-smelling towel from the laundry jauntily over my head, taking the cement walk that forked to the left and the guest dock—surely such distinctions as guests and help were suspended at this occasion, month and hour. If they weren't, they could damn well make a special dispensation for me.

Tut-tut-tut went the still-callused soles of my bare feet on the weathered dock boards. At the edge of the dock, I tore off my sweatpants and sweatshirt and leaped upward, tucking into a cannonball, anticipating the smash of the lake's cold fist.

* * *

Not even Ardis was in the kitchen. No matter. I went around turning on all the lights and putting down chairs and stools from the counters where we'd left them last night. I lit the steam table and ovens of the Garland ranges, lit the grill burners as well, and turned them down low. Then I cleared away debris I knew had been produced last night by the LaBaugh brothers, Roy and Gerald, legendary popcorn enthusiasts known for leaving their messes for others to clean up. And who better than me for the task? After all, I wasn't here to give away the bride or offer a homily.

I tossed the huge, charred saucepan in the pot sink, unburnt kernels and all, then panned three aluminum trays of bacon for the ovens, stirred up three quarts of pancake mix using Ardis' recipe from memory, and remembered to do one pan of Swift's sausage links.

At 7:45 I put the bacon and sausage in the oven, got out a big bowl of eggs, got out the spun aluminum egg pans, a small crock of melted butter and a can of Kaola Gold and put them on the serving table for Rex and Ardis.

Around five till, after I'd drained the bacon and sausage pans and put them in smaller pans on the top of the range above the grill to stay warm, and just as I was making an urn of coffee, Ardis and Rex came rather blearily in. Rex looked grim but determined to do whatever needed doing.

* * *

When the modestly-attended breakfast was over (there were only about fifteen guests and no more than half a dozen egg and pancake orders—morning-after tastes tended to run toward juice, coffee and toast), the supplies put away in the humming walk-in coolers, the meager pots and pans and dishes washed and put away, I stood on the back porch, wondering what to do next. Rex still looked a little green around the gills, and now slouched painfully and gratefully off toward his cabin for a little shuteye and recuperation.

When I heard the engine of the approaching car, I knew that somehow in the course of events this morning Yvonne and I would find or make a time and place for lovemaking; I was clearly out of my depth, but decided to say fuck it and let all considerations unrelated to our affair go jump—I'd try to sort it all out later, probably considerably later, and wouldn't worry about anything now except re-encountering Yvonne. I wondered if I were in love. If someone else described my own feelings to me, I supposed I might say it was so.

And sure enough, here came Yvonne in her spruce Chevy, turquoise and white finish glowing beneath a light coat of dust, pulling up behind the little cabin complex of which mine was a part (Donnie and Jack Tudd and the other young male guests, it turned out, were all staying in the dorm over the kitchen where the waitresses and salad girls ordinarily stayed in the summer, so Yvonne and I might have rattled the windows with cries from our love-nest last night had we wished), stopping decisively, stepping out, trim and lovely in jeans and blue turtleneck sweater—how nicely the faded denim cupped her ass.

Yvonne set a wad of flannel rags and a can of Simoniz on the car hood, looked over at me and smiled as I walked up; I smiled back, and we stood transfixed for several seconds as the hum of whatever it was we had commenced anew.

* * *

Washing the damn Chevy was too much trouble, we both agreed, so we went quickly round it with two huge beach towels Yvonne pulled from the trunk, rather jauntily snapping and rubbing the dust away. Then we set to work with damp rags, applying Simoniz, each of us doing one panel at a time, she on one side of the car, I on the other; by the time we'd finished waxing one panel, the previous one would have dried enough to be buffed. We worked quickly with the rags, waxing, rubbing, polishing, buffing, then waxing again. Occasionally we'd each send the other a quick bright glance.

It was hard work, and after a while Yvonne took off her turtleneck; beneath it she wore a bandanna shirt faded to magenta save under the arms where she'd sweated the fabric crimson. I followed the lift of her breasts as she worked with great concentration, using first one arm, then the other, then both, buffing away the white streaky glaze of Simoniz.

As she plied her rag carefully but energetically around one of the two rocket-shaped ornaments on either side of the hood I laughed foolishly, unable to tear my eyes from her strong active hands.

"Something strike you as funny?" She didn't look up but kept industriously after the phallic ornament.

"No, I'm just happy . . ."

"You have some things to be happy, about, do you?"

"Don't I?"

* * *

In a little over an hour we were almost done—only the hood, which I'd waxed, and one front fender, which she'd waxed, remained to be buffed. So we stopped and took our first real break and stood side by side, surveying the sparkling machine. We'd hardly spoken and hadn't touched since we'd begun work.

Then Yvonne stepped close to me and swung her hip against mine as schoolgirls sometimes do, knocking me off-balance. As I turned to repay her in similar fashion, HG's brown Ford wagon came rumbling down around the drive and pulled up beside Yvonne's Chevy. It was a V-8 stick shift—probably a pretty speedy machine. HG got out slowly, as if he were in various kinds of pain.

He wore a blue dress shirt and tie. His cuffless and striped flannel trousers were badly wrinkled and smirched with a gray smear of what looked like ashes, and yes, there was one of those little Ivy League belts at the back; still, he somehow managed to convey the impression that he could, if required, if someone offered, say, to publish his novel, shake himself off, straighten his shoulders, dash the wrinkles from his pants, and in spite of his present distress, be almost himself again.

He spoke to Yvonne without preliminaries: "I'm waiting for Gleason's to open down at Silver Bridge so I can get a bottle of cognac—Courvoisier, if they have it, if not, the hell with'em, if I can't have The Brandy of Napoleon I'll just have to go back with Old Grand-Dad . . . Christ it's hard to find good cognac in the boondocks . . ."

"How lovely. That's very helpful information."

"I was hoping we could have a little chat this morning . . ."

"Yes. When you dry out, I'll be happy to have a conversation with you." Tears stood in her eyes, but none leaked down her cheeks and her mouth was set in such a grim line she looked her age. She bit her lower lip and without explanation or the slightest glance at me dropped her flannel rag on the unpolished hood, wheeled and crossed the drive and disappeared into the pastry kitchen.

"Girls," HG said, turning to me, "pressure affects their kidneys. Always going potty. Whizzing. You know. Tinkling. So how've you been, there, Miller? How's the old kid surviving?" His handsome, haggard face was fish-belly white.

"Oh, can't complain, pretty well I guess . . ."

"You're in school somewhere I trust?"

"Yeah, at Ermine Falls in my last year—I'll probably go to Central State next year and major in English, Mister Goode."

"Excellent. But say, call me Harrison. Or better yet, HG. I guess I prefer HG, that's what my colleagues call me. Friends too, back when I had'em. Just another musty prof somewhere very near the end of the line, on the precipice of dissolution. Well, if you're an English major, in a sense we're colleagues, we're sort of in the same raft together. The two of us devoting our lives in one way or another to literature and all that, although as you can see, I also seem to have achieved a certain devotion to the Demon Rum at the moment. All temporary, I assure you, m'boy. You didn't ask how I'm doing, but I'll tell you: splendidly."

HG pulled a small curved silver flask from his hip pocket—a half-pint I judged—and elaborately unscrewed a cap chained to the body of the flask and offered it to me: "Yes, Miller, this is a little of the fabled Courvoisier, which I'm sure they won't have at the bridge. Have a belt? A little stirrup cup, so to speak?"

"Thanks, I can't HG . . . I'm in training, not to mention underage . . ."

"Sure." He upended the flask and the liquor went *gik-gik-gik* as it drained into his mouth. "You a writer, Miller?"

"Me? No . . . like I say, I'm planning on being an English major, but I never tried writing."

"Good. Don't ever get into writing, it'll buy you nothing but misery, unless of course you're content to be a dabbler like Yvonne, I mean the girl's bright and writes well and's got a modicum of talent but a few quiet stories will do the trick for her."

HG gave a quick sharp laugh like a fox's bark: "Of course she's brought some of her work out into the light while all mine lingers in gloom and shade: 'But here there is no light, Save what from heaven is with the breezes blown Through verdurous glooms and winding mossy ways,' as Keats put it . . ."

He took another pull from the flask and again offered it to me. He looked so bereft and alone I couldn't refuse; I even felt a twinge of something like protectiveness toward him. "Thanks, HG, don't mind if I do." And I took the small shiny flask, warmed by his hand, brought its small neck to my lips, faked taking a belt, then returned it to him. He smiled, gratified, and his deathly pallor abated a little. "Here's why you should avoid writing fiction, Miller: because you may fail. And let me tell you, and I think I speak with a certain authority here, there's no failure on earth which reaches one as deeply as artistic failure . . . you've no one else to fob things off on, it's oneself, oneself, oneself, who's not adequate to the task. Somerset Maughm in *The Summing Up* says of the writer, uh . . . 'life is a tragedy and by his gift of creation he enjoys the catharsis, the purging of pity and terror, which Aristotle tells us is the object of art . . . his griefs, humiliations, everything is transformed by his power into material and by writing it he can overcome it' . . . sounds great, eh? But there's just one major fly in the gazpacho, Miller . . . what if, say, whether by fate, luck, conspiracy, or the dynamics of the marketplace in that vale of anxiety in New York City they call publishing, your work remains forever prison-pent, forever entombed in a several pound mass of yellowing typescript? What then, Miller, what then? Of artist and manuscript? What if the writer's not strong enough or hasn't enough faith in his work to sustain him if he doesn't get some kind of reinforcement? Yes, I know all about Dickinson and Kafka and a lot of others. Maybe such a situation was good for Emily Dickinson or Kafka but what if you aren't Dickinson or Kafka? Am I in real pain, do you think? And say, wasn't it Dickinson who wrote: 'Men do not sham convulsion, Simulate a throe'? And what if you reach for it and it's not there? That was Cole Porter's biggest fear, y'know. The next idea. The next theme. The next line. Hell, the next fucking *word*!"

"Gosh, I dunno, HG. Maybe it's time to cut your losses and take a crack at something else?"

"*Excellent*! *Wha-hah-hah*!" It was the first time I'd heard his distinctive laugh since last summer: it was a breathy, rachety sound that reminded you of someone trying unsuccessfully to start a two-cycle engine, or perhaps of a window shade flying up and wrapping around itself. "You've put your thumb right on it, lad." His right hand was white from gripping his flask. He noticed me looking and relaxed his grip, letting color flow back into the hand. He smiled at me. "Thanks, Miller, you've been most helpful. Now I go in quest of Courvoisier—the brandy of Napoleon, *n'est-ce pas*? There are compensations in abnegation no matter what the bastards tell you. Hemingway doesn't call sauce the giant killer for nothing. Now that we've shared a drink, we're almost blood brothers—maybe we'll share another before we're done . . . or undone . . . so'd y'ever read Crane's *Maggie*: *A Girl of the Streets*, Miller me boy? No? Well, it's creaky and almost laughable with its 'deses' and 'dems' and 'doses' and its various faults—but it doesn't commit the cardinal sin, it's not dull and it sweeps you along with it in a series of riveting scenes"—*bam-bam-bam*—he struck the Chevy's hood with his fist three times for emphasis—"and it's literally *acrawl* with the kind of vitality that characterized Fitzgerald at his best. Crane's Jimmie Johnson, Maggie's brother—no, no, no, how'd I fuck *that* up, of course I mean *Pete*, Pete who deflowers Maggie and starts her on the famous garden path, roughneck Pete 'who seemed to strut standing still,' Pete with his 'bristling' mustache 'of short, wire-like hairs' . . . at one point this *tabula rasa* is capable of noting, 'Nuttin' lasts.' Or is it, 'Everyt'ing goes'? If Lady Yvonne were here and going me quote-for-quote, she'd prob'ly quote Shakespeare, 'Ripeness is all,' as Edward says in *King Lear* . . . I'm a Lowry man, m'self, Saint Malcolm knew the cure for alcoholism: gin and orange juice, *whah-hah-hah hawww* . . . as he says, 'the necessary, the therapeutic drink,' *whah-hah-hah* . . . furthermore, as Lowry pointed out, the *real* cause of alcoholism is 'ugliness and the complete baffling sterility of existence as it is *sold* to you' . . . d'j'you know the *Volcano* was rejected by twenty-eight editors, until finally Reynal and Hitchcock took mercy on the old sot? What a book! Sometimes I wonder if I married Yvonne 'cause that's the name of the Consul's wife in the *Volcano*. Listen to this last sentence of Chapter Two, Miller: 'In the dark tempestuous night, backwards revolved the luminous wheel' . . . *Whah-hah-hah* . . . or try this on for size: 'Ah none but he knew how beautiful it was, the sunlight, sunlight, sunlight flooding the bar of the El Puerto Del Sol, flooding the watercress and oranges, or falling like a lance straight into a block of ice—'"

HG was beginning to weave a little, even leaning up against Yvonne's Chevy, and he seemed to become aware of it as he studied my face. He consciously steadied himself, pulled himself erect and threw his narrow shoulders back. His brows knit. Then he stepped carefully back over to his Ford wagon, opened the driver's side, and lowered himself slowly into the seat, leaving the door open.

He looked up at me slyly: "The missus probably gave you the lowdown on me, din't she? Me'n my famous unpublishable novel? Clumsy-fucking-Partners? Well, what the hell, I'm not a writer. I'm a talker. That's how I make my living, you see, talking. Well, I see once again my lovely bride's gone 'cause she can't bear the sight of me with half a bun on. Well, fuck'er. We guys don't need women, right, Miller? Right? Not even the luscious Yvonne, me better 'alf, bejesus! *Whah-hah-hah* . . ."

"Right," I murmured.

"Sure you wouldn't like my last drop of Courvoisier?"

"No thanks."

"In that case, I'll have it myself . . ."

He held the flask, open, above his mouth and a last few drops ran into it. "Y'know, in his 'Crack-Up' essays, Fitzgerald, he who once wrote of the 'strength of a weak man,' says, 'Trouble has no necessary connection with discouragement—discouragement has a germ of its own, as different from trouble as arthritis is different from a stiff joint' . . . well, Miller, *mon vieux*, I . . . am . . . heavy, deep-down *discouraged* . . . though perhaps it's as Blake suggested, 'the fool who persists in his folly will become wise' . . ." He wriggled a bit as if to press himself deeper into the front seat of the Ford.

Keeping his watery intelligent pale blue eyes fixed on me, his right hand began to grope around the ignition and I noticed the key was in the switch and fastened there permanently with electrical tape—to cut down on losing it when juiced, I supposed.

The engine caught, throaty and powerful; the wagon had dual exhausts and what sounded like glasspack mufflers.

HG gave a wave from the window and drove away from the resort in low—I could hear him all the way out to the state road, the RPMs mounting on the straightaways, then slowing on the corners, when the mufflers popped like firecrackers.

I stepped back to Yvonne's Chevy and picked up the blue flannel rag Yvonne had left on the hood. Before I could turn I felt her hand lightly on my back—probably she'd been watching us from somewhere nearby, probably the pastry kitchen.

"God, HG makes me positively ill when he's like this . . ."

Yvonne's eyes were somber, bottomless. She gently pulled the rag from my suddenly lax hands and began to rub glazed wax away from the hood. Wanting to be close, I took my blue bandanna from my jean cut-offs and polished alongside her.

We worked in silence for perhaps ten minutes, our shoulders

occasionally touching, our thighs occasionally brushing. Then we were finished with both hood and front fender and she was standing close, putting her hand under my sweatshirt, kneading my upper back muscles. She withdrew it quickly, fearful we might be seen, and as if on signal we dropped our cloths and in half a dozen steps were on my doorstep. Yvonne cast a quick furtive look around to see if anyone might be spying on us. I looked myself: I saw nothing moving save shifting splotches of sunlight through the turning young maples around the cabin.

Once inside, she took charge again, thrilling me to the extent I shivered though I was still sweaty. She tugged my sweatshirt over my head, undid my shorts and let them fall, stepped back, thrust her jeans to her ankles and stepped on them, then went for her bandanna shirt—I admired her quick sure dexterity in precisely popping each small button from its hole—and in seconds we were on my bunk again, this time under the covers, shuddering and pressing together, all mouth and groin and tongue and I tore my Fruit of the Looms off to give my cock some room and pressed my other hand inside the back of her panties and between the warm moist hemispheres of her ass: and when she took my cock in her hand and I exploded over her in a gout: *oh, no, how could I have . . . How could I have* wasted *this—*

She pulled me close, laughing softly in my ear, nipping at it, then pressed her surprisingly cold nose into it, and I hugged her to me hard, pressing up against her sticky belly and panties.

Her hand was touching me again, slippery from my own semen, a sensation so erotic I achieved at least three-quarters of a blue-steeler in seconds. She kept at it, soft and girlish and giggly, kissing, rubbing, touching, squeezing . . . then she stopped.

"Whew!" She cast the light wool blanket covering us off on the floor, rolled me onto my back, and got astride me. She reached behind and undid her bra and her breasts swayed forward as she bent toward me so my mouth could reach her nipples with a small lift of my head. I was dizzy with excitement and disbelief: could she know I feared I was going to faint and miss it all?

She lifted her breasts from my face after each nipple had hardened under my tongue, took both my hands, and brought them forward so each held the waistband of her lilac lace-trimmed panties damp from my explosion, and I understood that I was to pull them down and off; but when I hesitated over my exact move, she reached behind impatiently, pulled them further down, shifting around a bit as she pulled them until they were around one ankle, where they remained.

She was immediately astraddle me again, leaning forward to kiss me, her tongue filling my mouth as she inserted me and I felt myself deep inside her and again close to fainting as she enveloped me further and her breasts were warm on my chest and her breath harsh in my ear. I could hear a sucking, sobbing sound not unlike butter being churned as we made love.

"Miller," she whispered as we ebbed, "quick, give me three adjectives that describe making love . . ."

I whispered back: "Another quiz? Okay, I'm game. Thrilling. Exciting. Exhilarating. Splendid."

"You get an almost perfect score," she whispered, then gave a little gasp as I began to harden inside her. "I love it that there's no hesitation in you . . . *oh*!"

Burying Elizabeth

June 1956

The backhoe ground forward like a tank up the steep grade of the rutted dirt road, Rex accommodating the jostling like a good horseback rider as the machine responded to his commands, tires biting and getting good purchase in the rocky soil. I trailed on foot.

Rex was more confident than he'd have been had he not had our dead milk cow, Elizabeth, in the forward scoop to give him ballast and diminish the danger of flipping the rig. The backhoe's rear digging bucket swayed before me like a monstrous claw.

I walked because Turner had once firmly told me I should never ride the backhoe with Rex when he was going up a grade. And though I figured that Elizabeth gave enough heft to the front to make riding safe, it was still just as well to not be where I might get in Rex's way if he needed to do something fast. I liked to watch him work the controls with his particular kind of speedy delicacy.

* * *

Elizabeth had died last night lying on the floor in the barn, her head still locked in the stanchion, legs splayed out and a mixture of shit and piss seeping into the gutter behind her. We hadn't moved her until tonight—it was around 7:30—because we'd wanted to wait until after work and do the job when it was cooler. She'd already begun to stink. Turner would just as soon have done it himself during the day, but he thought we wanted to do it ourselves out of affection or something for Elizabeth. Maybe we did.

*   *   *

In a flat clearing by our gone-awry orchard, Rex set the hydraulic struts that stabilized the machine and unlimbered the back claw. In about ten minutes he dug a grave, his hands flying over the rubber-knobbed handles that directed the claw, the machine bucking and shorting as digging went from light to heavy to light again. I sat cross-legged about twenty feet away, watching.

When he'd gotten the oval hole about five feet down, he swung the heavy claw to the right, then swung it back so it hit Elizabeth's corpse with a thump and the cow rolled over the edge and into the grave. Even above the backhoe's engine I could hear the sickening thud when she hit bottom.

I sprang to my feet—I'd somehow thought Rex would move the backhoe away and then we'd both sort of push her gently into her grave. This abrupt way of dealing with her irritated me and I stood glowering, hands in my jeans pockets, as Rex filled the grave. When the dirt began to mound above the ground, he used the backside of the claw to tamp it down.

*   *   *

When he was done, he pulled the claw up and secured it, retracted the hydraulic struts, then pulled the rig over to the road leading back down to our place. Then he shut the engine off, surprising me, since it was a diesel and sometimes hard to restart. The putrid stink of diesel exhaust lingered in the air.

Rex walked back to the filled-in hole and stood beside me, looking down at the raw ground. The silence felt good. Then I realized it wasn't silent at all, that the bugs and birds were all starting to make sounds again now that the ugly slam of the backhoe had quit.

"Good ole cow," Rex said thoughtfully, "Christ, we had her for . . . Jesus, over ten years, right, Miller? Gonna feel strange each of us not havin' to milk her every third day, I won't miss it but Turner might. I expect he sort of liked doing his share of the milking and looking out on our little pasture there and seeing her—liked hearing her, too, didn't he, when she was tearing up that green grass over there by the artesian well . . ."

"Yeah . . ." I wondered why he was telling me things I already knew. I'd pulled some honeysuckle off an old cedar fence that had once rimmed the orchard, and now I walked around a little, tamping the loose earth down here and there; then I tossed the stems and cloying flowers on the grave. They looked pathetic amid the dirt, pebbles, bits of broken shale, my sneaker prints and indentations from the backside of the claw. "Doc was telling me Neanderthals used to put flowers on the graves of their dead and also they'd keep and take care of their old and injured, you can tell that from their bones and implements where they dug up their camps and graves," I said.

"Yeah? Thought they was just a bunch of Alley Oops . . ."

"Well, they may have been that, too . . ."

"Well, this ain't the worst place to end up," Rex said, toeing a piece of shale away from the rim of the grave, then looking up into the star-peppered summer sky.

"Beats the fucking Clearwater Cemetery, that's for sure," I said. "What do you think of Turner's headstone?" Turner'd had it erected on our plot two months earlier.

"Can't say's I much like it," Rex said slowly, thoughtfully. "But hell, it's up to him, just like it would be to you or me, one of them things you make up your own mind about, no nevermind anybody else . . ."

"Well, I don't give a shit about the stone so much as what it says," I said. "That 1919-dash-19-blank really pisses me off . . . he thinks he knows for sure he's gonna die before the turn of the century . . . he'd only be eighty-one in 2000 . . ."

Rex said soberly, "Well, like I say, I don't much like it either, but it's one of them things you make your own mind up about . . ."

"Maybe you'n me ought to talk to him . . ."

"And say what? We don't like your tombstone, Pa, so whyn'tcha git rid of it?"

"Yeah. Something like that . . ."

"Jesus, remember Miller, he's paid him some stiff fucking dues for a little peace, goddamnit, and he's a right to do whatever the fuck he's a mind to, including how he arranges things for when he dies without us nagging . . ."

The phrase "when he dies" lingered on the night like a septic breeze and I suddenly wished I hadn't said anything.

"Ah, c'mon," Rex said crossly, "too much gloomy crap for one night, quitcher belly-achin', Christamighty, so the old cow's dead, we're all together now, ain't we, and more or less okay, and hey: now you're a man 'cause you got laid last night. There's lots of other stuff coming to you, pal, don't do any good to get all bogged down with this death crap . . ."

I wanted badly to acquiesce, but something turned obstinate in me: "I don't give a fuck, I think I'll ask him to get rid of the fucking stone and he can do it or not do it as he sees fit. I got a right or two, too, y'know . . ."

Rex was silent a few moments, then said: "Okay, if you want to go ahead and do that and he asks me, I'll second your motion. Now let's see if I can start the backhoe up, sonofabitch gets cranky sometimes, probably should've let her idle, didn't make no difference to Elizabeth anyhow."

"Yes it did," I said.

"Okay, it did."

An owl's *whoooo-hoooooo* augmented other sounds of night: peepers, leg fiddlers, all keening.

"I'll ride alongside you on the way back down," I said. "If you're gonna kill yourself, I might's well croak too."

Chapter Seven

Around 11:00 the event that had brought bride and groom, guests, relatives and help together began with a wheezy inspiration from an antique organ; then Mendelsohn flooded the main room of the Lodge, which was more than adequate for the gathering since all the bridge tables that ordinarily cluttered the space had been stored in the pavilion. We all stood.

The small organ, a LaBaugh heirloom, and according to Ardis, over a hundred years old, was tucked by the stairway that conveyed you to and from the upstairs rooms (occupied during the season by "transients," mostly friends or relatives of long-time clientele popping in for a weekend) and was played by Daphne Redpath. The organ was not much larger than a small writing desk and as severe, thin-lipped Daphne pumped the pedals ever more vigorously and the chords deepened, a thin dust rose from it and drifted upward, sparkling like mica through a parabola of sunshine cast from a fanlight over the west door. Shadows from the bars of the fanlight fell on a worn Oriental carpet before the audience and looked like hairy spider legs.

Though you could hear the straining of the organ mechanism over the music, it was nonetheless stirring, and the room's many wooden surfaces gave the rich bass notes splendid resonance.

Christ, I thought, could I ever end up in front in one of these things? It was a thought both frightening and thrilling, and I reminded myself that if marriage were a half safe bet, Turner would likely have remarried.

The svelte and mild-faced maid of honor, Bettina Lourde, preceded by two young girls in taffeta related to the LaBaughs, tossing flower petals and giggling, descended the stairs.

And now, most of the audience of perhaps thirty-five grasped the backs of the creaking wooden fold-up chairs of the people in front of them as the familiar wedding march filled the room, some craning their heads as Clover LaBaugh appeared at the top of the stairs on the arm of Roy LaBaugh, the slightly older brother who didn't smoke and, a college administrator, was thought to be a model of probity, just as Gerald ("the gadfly") had a reputation for being flighty and frivolous.

I was on the last row of chairs with Rex on my left and Christy Bannerman on my right; we were the furthest removed from the southwest corner where the ceremony was about to be performed; however, our vantage gave us probably the best wide-angle view of the proceedings.

As Clover and Roy LaBaugh moved down the carpeted stairs toward Jeff Budlong and Jerry Smink, stationary in the chosen corner, I heard a sigh or two, then some other kinds of liquid sibilance, in spite of the organ. A contagion of modest weeping commenced and slowly but steadily spread among the women, most notably the older ones (the younger, I suspected, were fearful of their makeup). Even Christy was blinking a little and dabbing quickly at her eyes with a lace-trimmed hankie. I managed to get a quick look at Yvonne, standing up with her family and next to HG in the first row of seats. For the second time since I'd laid eyes on her, her ordinarily animated face could be said to have a stony cast.

Harrison Goode stood sweating in a tan gabardine suit, repeatedly swallowing, occasionally lifting a trembling hand to his throat to fiddle with his tie, all signs of someone badly in need of a drink. Yvonne seemed wary that he might sway toward her and accidentally touch her.

I was glad to have the most obscure seat in the house for as soon as the ceremony was over I planned to slip away unnoticed, retire to my cabin, and brood over tactics and strategy on how and when Yvonne and I might next be together. Wasn't that a lover's job?

* * *

By now Mrs. Bentley Hemmings, Mrs. Wendall Gallagher, Mrs. Millard Wahoola, the buxom Gloria Wahoola and Mrs. Kent Carrothers were all rather leaky, while there was a bright almost haggard look of excited yearning on the faces of the younger and "eligible" females, who like their elders dabbed at their eyes and occasionally, modestly blew their noses with insignificant force into hankies.

Like me, Rex wore chinos and white shirt and a collegiate crew-neck sweater. I was happy to see we weren't the only ones without coats and ties; it seemed permissible for the younger to be casual—the rustic setting seemed to invite if not require it. I doubted anyone would notice I wore tennis shoes, nor care if they did.

Clover had by now been escorted by brother Roy to the southwest corner to stand by Jeff Budlong and Jerry Smink.

The organ ceased and we all sat.

There were murmations from bride and groom interspersed with bass rumblings of the Presbyterian minister's sonorous public voice as the marriage vows were exchanged. It was hard from where I sat to make out more than an occasional word.

Sunlight streamed through the windows making Clover's dress almost luminous; Jeff Budlong's chestnut crew cut caught the sun so he seemed to have a kind of halo and Jerry Smink's hair turned bright copper in the buttery light.

I was gratified that Donnie Redpath, sitting two rows ahead and to my right, looked as miserable as his shit-faced condition of the previous evening had suggested he might be—in fact he and Rex looked equally hung-over.

Then I noticed a girl sitting next to Donnie—Lindsay Noel, whose father, Vernon, lived in Ermine Falls and ran the Oldsmobile agency in Skeegemog; she'd started at Ermine Falls school as a freshman last year but had left quickly at the end of September and gone to University High in Ann Arbor where she had an aunt. She wore a light blue-and-white finely-checkered dress with a white collar and a beige cardigan and was beautiful: her thin somewhat angular limbs were still golden from summer sun and her shoulder-length auburn hair looked made of burnished metal. Something about her made my heart contract though she seemed the antithesis of lush Yvonne (my lover, I reminded myself).

I remembered catching a glimpse of Lindsay last August during a rain. Rex and I had brought a cord of cut and split fireplace wood over in Turner's pickup and, while Rex ran down to the office in the downpour, I had watched from the truck window through a curtain of water as Lindsay Noel and two other girls about her age in shorts and halters giggled and pranced and shrilled under streams of rain sluicing from a broken eave trough over the kitchen, shampooing and rinsing their hair, angular and awkward as mantises.

"Jesus, Miller," I told myself, "you're a . . . a caution. Here you are just four months into being nineteen and you've been making love almost continuously to a brilliant and extremely delectable older woman, and suddenly in the distance you spot this thin, short-titted and probably snotty cutie pie Lindsay Noel again and your heart goes pitty-pat. What's the deal here, Miller?"

And what was it Rex had told me last year? He'd been doing a stint as janitor at the Ermine Falls School while Mr. Peet recovered from the flu and he'd caught a backwoods asswipe named Basil Purvis trying to force himself on Lindsay in the athletic equipment room off the gym and had run Basil off. Then he'd helped Lindsay slip away from school to go home—and she never returned. Went to Ann Arbor and now she'd reappeared and was here with her older friend Christy Bannerman. I'd been only vaguely interested then, had only half-listened while Rex spun his yarn.

But as my glancing recollection of Lindsay and my startlement at seeing her here ebbed, I thought of Yvonne, of her plenitude and expertise, and my blood stirred quickly back toward her until I wanted her again and again, and as soon as possible, and surely the opportunity was somewhere in close by—at hand—and if it weren't I'd make it so—

All were rising again and I tardily imitated the others: the marriage was accomplished and Clover swept back her diaphanous veil as if brushing away a fly and Jeff Budlong took her in his arms and to a dignified clapping and a few hoots and whistles crushed her to him. Flashbulbs popped.

Rex and I slipped away as congratulations, and kisses and more weeping resonated behind us—we headed to the dining room for a quick look at how the reception preparations were going. An outfit from Traverse City, DeYoung Catering, was doing the reception and our work was basically over, save perhaps policing up the kitchen in the morning: the help were at liberty.

* * *

Rex and I reached the dining room before anyone else. Behind us the wedding party and guests were gradually reassembling outside the Lodge and in moments cheers arose, probably as the newlyweds were pelted with rice.

We climbed the steps up to the dining room's front portico, crossed it, and strolled into the dining room as if we'd just popped in from St. Louis or Cincinnati or Detroit to lend the weight of our presence to the doings.

We were a bit surprised: this was of a different order than the relatively simple fare we'd fed the group the night before and for breakfast. Not only were the smorg tables used but a couple more fold-up tables had been brought in the caterer's two white vans and all were now covered with tablecloths so brilliant it seemed they must have some source of illumination hidden in their thread. And they were being laden with food, trays of highly garnished almost miniature sandwiches without crusts skewered with toothpicks with gay little paper frills on their ends and other gew-gawish dainties and morsels. Back in the kitchen, ovens in the pastry and main kitchens were going and most of the available counter space by the ranges was covered with pans either just out of or shortly to go into the oven—little sausages in crusts, various seafood items, other items I couldn't identify. I wondered where the cake was.

"Holy shit," Rex called from the room that housed the walk-ins, "come take a look at this, Miller . . ."

He'd opened the door of the meat cooler and stood looking in. I joined him and gave a low whistle: there was barely room for a person to get into the cooler and maneuver around the shoulder-high cases of Taylor Brothers champagne. I counted them: twenty-four, each with six bottles. One hundred and forty-four bottles, or about three apiece for every man, woman and child on the Champs, including help.

"Please step aside, fellas," said a middle-aged, gray-mustached man done up in blazing white trousers, tunic and a chef's toque, and I felt an urge to laugh aloud at his pretentious garb and manner—after all, the son-of-a-bitch was about matters no more complex than heating crap in ovens, then garnishing and serving it. Nevertheless, Rex and I stepped back obligingly and watched him remove a couple of aluminum trays of something from the overhead racks where ordinarily watermelons were kept during the summer.

I noticed one bottle was already missing from the top case of champagne, so I reached over and plucked another out. "Might's well save us one for later," I said. "For you and me."

Rex shrugged.

He really wasn't very interested in all this. When his eyes widened at whatever he was seeing over my shoulder, I turned: Christy Bannerman stood before the steam table looking sad and pretty, her large dark eyes wide with something I couldn't read—but didn't have to since they were fixed on Rex, and whatever it was, it wasn't my problem.

Christy drew her underlip between her front teeth and I took that as my cue: "See ya in a while," I said, turning toward the door that let onto the cement drive, "I'm gonna go over and lie down for a bit, maybe take a nap . . . see you a little later on . . ."

Wasn't that a flicker of gratitude in Rex's eyes?

Before leaving, I took a quick look back through the swinging doors out into the dining room and was just in time to see two of the caterer's white-clad flunkies carrying a large, four-tiered wedding cake through the front doors to the accompaniment of clapping. I ducked quickly back into the kitchen and left through the pastry kitchen so as not to intrude on Rex and Christy.

* * *

As soon as I entered my cabin, I stuck the fifth of champagne I'd appropriated under the bunk, and as I did I heard the sound of Yvonne's '57 Chevy accelerating out the drive at a pretty good clip. For some reason her absence made me feel sleepy; I had half an impulse to open the champagne—something I'd never tasted—and have a couple of slugs just for the novelty. Then I rejected the idea—Yvonne might come back soon and I'd no wish to piss her off. There was plenty of time coming when Rex and I could sample the stuff.

Still, I was thirsty so I decided to nip back over to the kitchen and maybe find some orange juice in the vegetable walk-in.

I went into the cooler, closing the door behind me, and poked around until I found a half-full quart. I took a long drink right away, but before I could push the door open, the door to the adjoining meat cooler where the champagne was stored opened.

"Rex," I heard Christy say clearly, for the coolers were open overhead, "Come here, I have something for you . . ."

There was the sound of the door closing, then silence; I thought about nipping out my door and getting away from the kitchen before they were able to see who'd been in the adjoining cooler, then decided to wait them out.

"Rex . . . you *know* you have a real appeal for almost every part of me . . . but I've been hurt before and so I'm trying to be careful, Rex, but I *do* like you a lot and . . . if you're willing to take things slow and not make too many *demands* . . ."

"Well, I thought you and Donnie . . ."

"Oh, Donnie's *such* an asshole . . . Rex, I mean with us, I'd like for you to write me when I'm back at school. I think people communicate who they really are better through letters than by any other means, and I'd just *love* to correspond with you . . . if you're willing, that is . . ."

"Correspond," Rex repeated slowly, trying out the alien word. "That's fine for the future, Christy, but how about now—I've got one powerful urge to kiss you and hold you tight and be with you. C'mon over to my cabin for a few minutes, then we'll head back to the reception . . ."

They left quickly, and after a short interval I followed with my orange juice. I was ravenous, but my hunger didn't seem to require slaking as did my thirst.

When I got back to my cabin I drained the rest of the orange juice, skinned down to my Fruit of the Looms, and crawled inside the tightly made bed. Surely this was what being in the womb was like, I thought as my cold toes wriggled into folds of sheet. All I really knew of my mother, though, was that her name had been LaVern. There was no rule to that effect, but she was the one topic neither Turner nor Rex nor I ever broached, all of us in a kind of cabal, always quickly shying away from the subject if ever it got close.

* * *

Yvonne and I were together in bed, entwined. My eyes were shut and she was naked against naked me, but she felt different, her limbs were harder, thinner, her breasts smaller, her nipples smaller and hard as acorns, then a sharp elbow dug into my midriff and I opened my eyes and looked into the level slate-gray eyes of Lindsay Noel. "Miller," she whispered, and I awoke with a start, in a state of desire so advanced I didn't doubt a single stroke of my hand would have sent globs spurting into the bedclothes. "Lindsay," I murmured, and then I was fully awake: "Yvonne," I said slowly, softly, insistently: "Yvonne."

I was hungry, wished I'd at least gotten myself some of that wedding cake.

Cultivation

June 1953

It was a Tuesday in June and since school'd been out, I'd been minding the shop for a few hours every now and then when both Rex and Turner were gone. Today, they'd taken our five-ton truck over to the foundry in East Jordan, laden with probably a hundred radiator cores with the steel housings knocked off, and probably close to sixty old batteries, not to mention a bunch of engine blocks and other items, along with several hundred pounds of lead pipes they'd found in the bed of a wrecked truck they bought from a private party—"Probably stolen from someplace I expect, but what the hell," Turner'd observed. "Nobody to play good neighbor to, so I guess it's 'finders' keepers'."

For the first time, I did what Turner'd always told me I could do when I was on the place alone and felt like it, turned the OPEN sign around on the window of the shop door so it read CLOSED, and locked up.

* * *

I biked the mile and a half down to the Knowles' farm, pulled up in the driveway leading past their gas storage shed, and pedaled up to the barnyard. I could see Doc off on the southwest cornfield guiding a cultivator pulled by Dandy and Belle, their two draft horses. It was like looking at some kind of living painting: earth, Doc, horses, far-off hills, sun, white puffy clouds scudding briskly through a deep blue sky.

I thought of times riding the bus to school when I'd see the Knowles' team in profile in the pasture, the nose of one rubbing against the hind quarters of the other, both of them otherwise motionless except for tails flicking every now and then. That made me think of the rear part of the MacReady house they called "up above," a kind of attached attic, workshop and storage area built over Sonney's root cellar. It was mostly devoted to trunks of old clothing; bundled, decades-old magazines (*Argosy*), antique tools, festoons of dried halves of morels strung like Christmas popcorn, furniture and other items. Among such things were two fringed rawhide harnesses that Sonney's mules, Jenny and Maud, had worn to shoo horseflies as they worked the fields decades before Rex and I were born.

* * *

I leaned the bike against the fence, opened the gate into the barnyard, went on past the barn, climbed the fence and went through an overgrown lot until I came to the field where Doc and the team were at work.

Here came Doc now, hands on the cultivator, one rein over each shoulder with both tied together at his back. He wore jeans but his feet were bare. His red hair glowed like copper in the sun.

"Whoa up! Whoa!" Doc brought the horses to rest—Dandy, Doc's favorite, was considerably bigger than Belle, but they seemed to work well together and must have adjusted to their disparity of strength and size over the years. Doc draped the reins over the cultivator handles.

"Whew," he said, coming up to me, wiping his hands on the back of his jeans, then mopping his face with a bandanna, "gonna be hottern's a bitch come late afternoon—hey, maybe when I get this done how's 'bout we ride our bikes out to the bridge and see what's going on—I only got about twenty minutes more here and then, if I can get the team unharnessed and cooled down a bit and in the barn before Odell gets back and dreams up something new to do, maybe we can make our escape . . ."

"Sounds good to me . . . say, Doc, y'know, I was thinking. Here I live on what was a farm out here in the country but I've scarcely held a pair of reins in my hands . . . 'bout our only farming is our milk cow and Turner's vegetable garden."

"Want to take a crack at it? Easy as rolling off a log, this's just a run before planting, don't have to take a whole lot of pains with it. Tell you what, I'll walk over with you and you can just pick up both reins, put'em over your head, give the horses a little *chik-chik*, then say 'Giddap' and give'em just a tiny little shake-slap with the reins and you're off . . . see, keep'em straight as you can, hold your cultivator steady but loose and even and watch out for big rocks, don't need to press down hard or nothing, the cultivator's weight'll do it. You get to the end of the row and holler '*Haw*!' for left . . . and pull easy on the left rein and just follow'em easy on around and make your turn . . . pull the rein a little harder if they're taking the turn too wide. But don't worry, there's nothing to mess up. That's about all there is to it. C'mon, I'll give you a hand at first . . ."

* * *

Doc and Tucker's old man Odell hadn't gotten back by the time we finished the last bit of cornfield, so Doc brought the horses into the farmyard and over to the cement livestock trough for big, long drinks. Then he took off both harnesses ("Thanks, but it'll be faster if I do it alone, Miller.") in the barnyard and took them into the barn and hung them on pegs. Then, while I held the halters of each horse in turn, Doc slopped three milk pails of water over each and we worked on them with metal curry combs. Then Doc dried them lightly with a big orange and blue beach towel and put them in their stall. I rubbed Dandy's nose before we left.

* * *

We biked down to my place and found Turner and Rex were still gone so I ran up and got my tennis shoes, swimming trunks, and a little money. Then Doc and I were off, dressed identically in jeans and T-shirts, heading into Ermine Falls with our trunks and towels in our baskets. From there we'd follow Aarwood Road three miles out to Silver Bridge, where we could hang around, look over the resorters, and swim in Silverfish Lake's public area by the swing bridge if we wanted to. We could change into our suits in the bathroom of the Gulf station.

I thought how good it always felt to ride back from the bridge with your wet bathing suit on and your jeans and towel in your basket. And it was great to feel warm water suddenly trickle out of your ears as you pumped the pedals.

It felt great to be doing this particular thing on this particular day with this particular guy who was my best friend after Rex. But I was still in a bit of a daze from the twenty minutes (or thereabouts) I'd spent behind Dandy and Belle: never had horses seemed bigger to me than when I was behind them, gripping the surprisingly unwieldy cultivator and trying to keep it straight. The reins were tied together as Doc'd left them over my head, the ends trailing down my sweating back.

After a while, I'd been able to get the hang of bringing off a pretty decent left turn, but what thrilled me was commanding the two huge blindered, docile animals with their enormous strength. It was so different from a machine's, so rich with horse-scent, sending back an occasional rippling then sputtering horse-fart, and then the feel of the damp dark earth on my bare feet and the sharp feel of the occasional stone and the breeze playing on my bare skin and the sounds from the harness, horsecollar, hames and the clink of singletrees.

* * *

We stopped for the moment at Ernie's Sinclair station in Ermine Falls. On our bikes but not moving, we kept balanced with one foot on the concrete cube by Ernie's that had a pipe coming out of it and then an air hose coiling from it and suspended from a hook on the pipe.

"What?" I'd been thinking about the horses and missed what Doc'd said.

"I said, long's we're in town, wanta swing past Carstairs' and see if Larry'd like to go on out to the bridge with us? He's probably home . . ."

"Yeah, okay. Y'know, I was just thinking about cultivating with your team . . . Jesus, you can really kinda lose track of everything but what you're doing, can't you . . . I always liked horses, but never had anything to do with them . . . Dandy's sure a strong horse . . ."

"Yeah, he's a good old horse," Doc said. "'Course he's getting up there, he's close to twenty so he ain't got too many more good years in front of him . . ."

"Well, after that it'll be like in that song Sonney taught me that we used to sometimes sing together for Pearl, 'Old Faithful,' right? And I sang, 'And when your roundup days are over, there'll be pastures wide with clover, for you, Old Faithful pal o'mine' . . ."

I lifted my right hand from the handlebar and smelled the horse and leather scents I'd acquired, and it suddenly occurred to me where I saw the beach towel Doc used on the team: lying on the guest dock at Les Champs du Roi when we'd ridden out there about a week ago. Doc must have stuffed it on the sly into the knapsack he wore that day.

Since Doc hadn't said anything, I looked over at him and saw a pained expression on his face. When he saw me looking, he said, "Sure, I expect that's what'll happen." Then he looked up into the cloud-puffed blue sky.

"Damn right," I said, "Nobody's gonna let a good old horse like Dandy work his ass off and then send 'im off to the glue factory . . ."

Doc didn't answer.

"Yeah," I said. "Let's go get Larry Carstairs, see if he wants to come . . . he'll want to, but the question is, will his old lady let 'im?"

"Yeah," Doc said, "Let's go find him."

We both pushed off from the concrete cube with the air hose and headed Larry's way.

Above us the fat clouds tore through the blue sky at a good clip.

Chapter Eight

The sound of Yvonne's Chevy pulling up in the spot where earlier in the day we'd waxed it awakened me. I could hear a formal-sounding bass voice on the radio as the car sat idling. Probably she was listening to news—perhaps like Turner, she was addicted to the practice.

I was warm and comfortable, snuggled into the covers on the narrow bunk (what exciting things you could do on this modest space!) and again I briefly wondered about our mother who had deserted Turner and Rex in me in 1940. All I really knew of her beyond her name, LaVern, was that she had remarried and lived in northern Georgia—married to the truck driver she'd left Turner, Rex and me for. Once, Ruth Ann Perkins had startled me by asking if I ever considered going to Georgia and looking her up. "Christ," I told Ruth Ann, "I'd pay money to never ever have to lay eyes on her." But still I wondered.

Yvonne silenced the engine and radio simultaneously.

I looked around, feeling a bit groggy though I had another raging boner; and I wondered if it might be attributable to Yvonne's proximity or to my earlier, near wet dream which had had Lindsay Noel as its source of stimulation. And why should a single look at that skinny, stuck-up bitch set off such a reaction in me? Doubtless Yvonne had a handy quote or two from Donne or Keats or Yeats or Chekhov or somebody that would explain it all.

I'd left my inner door open. When I looked out through the screen door, the light had that particular falling quality of an autumn afternoon. I guessed I'd slept for forty-five minutes or so. Then Yvonne pushed the screen door open and came in. She didn't bother shutting it.

She again wore well-faded Levi's, this time a pair with rolled cuffs, and a green plaid flannel shirt too big for her with huge sleeves rolled up to her elbows. I'd noticed she seemed to have a fondness for dark green, which seemed to darken the hue of her already dark eyes and enhance that sprite-like quality that belied her true sumptuousness.

Without a word she came over and sat on the edge of the bed, more or less pinning me beneath the covers. She leaned over and very slowly and very gently brought her lips to press lightly on mine; the tip of her tongue slightly parted my lips and delicately touched my tongue.

But when I got my arms loose from the constricting covers and reached for her, she got quickly up and stood just out of range, arms akimbo, fists balled on her hips: "No, my dear, a little circumspection, if you please. We might just be tempting fate if we attempted a tryst under cover of daylight twice in the same day . . . my, didn't you have a nice long rest . . . feel invigorated by events, do you?"

"What time's it?"

"About 5:30. That's why the air, in fact this very afternoon has this . . . sort of *crepuscular* quality . . ."

"I can see that's another one I'll have to look up—should have brought my dictionary. Christ Almighty! So I've been asleep for close to four hours . . ."

"So you have, my dear . . . after all, you're a growing boy. But, poor fellow, you do have this *ravenous* older lover who keeps draining your vitality . . . oh, guess where I was while you were getting your rest and the others were swilling champagne and gobbling those hideous finger sandwiches and ughsome baked things and wedding cake? The cake was quite splendid, by the way. I hope you had some. I personally didn't bother."

"I only got a glimpse of the cake as they were packing it through the doors of the dining room. But I'll bite—where you been?"

"I guess I should have brought you some. Cake. Well, as for me, I've been out driving thither and yon. First, I was in Deer Rapids, then I was in Northport—driving, you see, always helps me clarify my thoughts—and I finally ended up in Petoskey and went into this little lapidary shop looking for something for the man who has everything. And guess what, I found something I thought appropriate for you. I love giving gifts. I've loved giving myself to you. And so, I got a little remembrance that seemed just the thing for you. Here. It's supposed to bring you luck . . ."

She unbuttoned the pocket over her left breast, extracted something and handed it to me. I held it in my palm and regarded it with wonder—a highly-polished oval Petoskey stone that gleamed like oiled mahogany in the dim light; the dark spots, called "eyes," were almost black, and I nearly gasped at the resemblance in shape and structure it bore to the one I carried in my pocket—one Turner'd smoothed into an oval shape on a piece of carborundum, then buffed on a cloth wheel with jeweler's rouge. I'd carried it in my pocket next to my jackknife for three years and by now its surface had become dulled and slightly pitted, though, of course, I could easily restore it if I chose.

"I can see sometime I'm going to have to equip you with a timepiece . . . as I say, I *love* buying and giving things to people I like, and after all"—the darkening of her eyes made her look more serious than affectionate—"you *are* my lover, are you not, at least until tomorrow . . ."

Tomorrow! "We'll be together again even after this is over, I'll see to it," I said firmly, maybe even grimly.

"I love to hear you say that, and I like your decisive tone. Maybe you're right, but for the moment let's just . . . live the moment as Eastern thought suggests, let's just exist in the so-called Eternal Present: no dipping into the past to make projections into the future. I must remember to send you a book of Krishnamurti's. I think *The First and Last Freedom* would be the perfect volume for you . . . I'm digressing, aren't I? Well, when one's lover is lying probably naked or nearly so under the covers before one, it's nearly enough to distract one . . ."

"Thank you," I said as the stone warmed in my palm. "And I'll . . . cherish this. I have something for you, too—I'll see you have it before you leave . . ."

"Dear one, there's no need for any sort of reciprocal response with me . . ." Her look darkened.

So how about this for a response, Yvonne: I reached out quickly for her with both hands, but again she stepped quickly back a pace, eluding me; my fingertips tingled with want. "It'll be dusk in about an hour or so," I said.

"I s'pose . . ." Her eyes retained that somber, unfathomable look, deepened by her green shirt, as though she were brooding on some unpleasant topic even as another part continued a lover's badinage. "What do you know about Petoskey stones?"

"Not much, except you find them mostly around Grand Traverse and Little Traverse Bays, and they're fossils of some kind . . ."

"Yes. Well. That's so. You also can find them in other counties and places in Michigan, of course, but the most beautiful come from the two Traverse Bays and the best ones have this kind of rich caramel color. They're a coral called *Hexagonaria*—from around 400 million years ago, give or take a few million, in the Devonian . . . a time of really odd fishes—bony ones, and spiders and millipedes. The first amphibians were just beginning to emerge and there were vascular plants, but no flowers, and so everything was green. It was a monochrome world, Miller, until the Cretacious when angiosperms began to develop and transform the world in a thousand important ways: Can you imagine a world with no flowers? Maybe I'll send you Loren Eisely's *The Immense Journey* along with the Krishnamurti—Eisely's a sort of wonderful neo-Thoreauvian. Anyway, there were these *Hexagonaria* coral, which later on were covered by mud and petrified . . . the dark round spots they call eyes are really where *Hexagonaria* took in food. The mouths filled with silt and mud and became mineralized. Those striations you see radiating from the eyes were actually tentacles. Living creatures, Miller, from so long ago we really can't *conceive*—I mean in geologic time we haven't been here even a tick of a *second*. My God, three-quarters of the earth's life is from around five thousand million years ago up to—let's not quibble—say, around six hundred million years ago. God! 'We live in the flicker,' as Conrad's Marlow says in *Heart of Darkness*. We're all just dying animals, aren't we? Doesn't it all just fill you with a somber wonder? I've always loved Petoskey stones so much more than trilobites or horned coral or anything else, they're just *so* beautiful . . ."

I knew I could never exchange her stone for the one Turner had ground by hand and polished for me and which was almost identical to the one he carried. But I'd meant it. Her gift was beautiful and indeed I'd cherish it. In fact, I'd probably never be able to touch it without getting a boner. I'd keep it in my cigar box of mementos and odds and ends at home.

I knew exactly what I would give to her—in fact, I had it in my shaving kit, where I carried it as a kind of back-up lucky piece to my Petoskey stone.

"They do," I said.

"What?"

"Petoskey stones. They fill me with wonder, always have even if I didn't know much about them."

"You thought it'd be dusk before too long? You're right. But now I've got to run and see what mischief HG's up to. But somehow I've the feeling we'll run into each other a little later on . . ."

"I can't think why we wouldn't . . ."

"Let's hope so . . ."

"*I* certainly hope so . . ."

"Me too."

Money

September 1946

On a bright Saturday in early fall of 1946, Turner took me along with him in the pickup when he went in to the Vulcan State Bank to deposit several days' money. He'd had a good week and had sold two rebuilt truck transmissions.

But, why did he want me to go inside with him? I'd sooner have waited in the pickup and watched people come and go. Besides, I didn't much like the bank's kind of floor-wax-old-socks-dentist's-office smell.

While I stood looking around, Turner talked to Guy Belcher, the vice-president, at one of the cashier windows.

All of a sudden I noticed they were both watching me, smiling.

Guy Belcher was a friendly guy about Turner's age with a good head of gray-shot hair, and now the both of them were giving me a look like a kid'd give you while his pal was bending down behind you so he could give you a sudden shove and send you ass over teakettle. I didn't always get what Turner found so damn funny, whether it was something he read in the paper or heard on the radio or saw in real life.

Sometimes when we'd go to Traverse City, Turner'd park on East Front Street rather than going to the municipal parking lot. When it came time to leave, we might just sit there for half an hour before we left, looking at the people going both ways on the street. Turner and Rex always found the variety of passers-by entertaining and sometimes they'd smile, nudge one another and point out some goofy-looking person. But all it did for me was make me antsy and eager to be back home—all the damn cars and the sun shining on bright things and people, people all over the place, up and down the sidewalks as if they had to get where they were going or die.

Now Turner drew back away from the cashier's slot and Guy beckoned me to him with a finger. He held a scrap of paper in his other hand. Maybe it had something to do with the Savings Bonds that Rex and I gave to from our allowances and doing chores like gathering walnuts or fetching the cow.

I went over.

Guy Belcher, looming above me, leaned forward a bit so he could look down on me, and I smelled the tobacco on his breath coming down to meet me. His fat, black-rimmed glasses made him look like a teacher, but then a shock of black-gray hair fell over one of his eyes and he looked sort of like an old kid. The little shelf in front of the teller's place where people put their passbooks and other stuff was about even with my head.

"Remember you was telling me you didn't believe there was such a thing as a hundred dollar bill?" Turner asked behind me. "How you said nobody's fool enough to make a single piece of paper worth that much 'cause somebody could steal it so easy? That if you had one then, why then anybody could just reach out and grab it and run and you'd be screwed, whereas a whole hundred dollars in ones'd be a big fistful and hard to get away with? Well sir, me'n him got something to show you. Okay, Guy, you hand it to him and I'll sidle toward the door in case he makes a break for it. He's a slippery one, a reg'lar Pretty Boy Floyd . . ."

And Turner edged off toward the door, where he waited, grinning.

I turned back to Guy and he handed the piece of paper down to me. It had an olden times guy's face and name on it. Its corners claimed it was a hundred dollars but I didn't really believe it. They must be playing a joke on me.

I turned the bill over in my hands and rubbed it between my thumb and forefinger like Pearl did with cloth when she was mending things. I brought it to my nose and sniffed the money smell of it. I thought of all you could buy with a hundred dollars. Hundreds of ice cream cones, maybe thousands. Cartons of cigarettes. Maybe you could buy a horse or a cow or a car or a washing machine or a deer rifle or a shotgun or a bus ticket to Alaska. You could get a brand new Spalding first baseman's glove like

Rex's and have enough left over for eight or nine more. Sonney and Pearl could have their house insulated. They could lay in enough flour, and cornmeal, and sugar and fuel oil to tide them over a winter and still have enough to go see a Roy Rogers movie or two in Skeegemog like we did about every other weekend during the war. If I had $100, I'd give it to them.

"Huh?" I'd got so interested in figuring and imagining I'd missed what Turner'd said from his post by the door.

"I said, how's about it there, John Dillinger, you going to grab the cash and make a run for it? . . ."

He stepped a little away from the front door to give me a sporting chance.

Two middle-aged men in suits and ties at the other two cashier windows turned to watch, smiling.

Maybe I *could* fool Turner, walk over to him holding the bill out to him, and when he reached for it I'd suddenly duck down and shoot quick between his legs and out the door—

—A chill struck me as I thought where I'd be when I made it past the door and found myself standing outside in the blazing sunlight, alone, no place to go, no place to run to, no home or father or brother to return to. I'd be just another crook on the lam, like they said in movies. I'd have no friends and be chased by posses of assholes.

I got a little dizzy and dropped the bill on the floor and just stood there weaving around. Guy Belcher quickly disappeared from his cashier's window and came around from behind the counter, but he was beaten there by Turner.

My father dropped to his knees before me and took a shoulder in each hand, his eyes filled with what looked like pain and sadness. He hugged me to him and my face pressed up against his bristly one.

In a moment or two he put a finger under my chin and lifted my face up so I had to look him in the eyes, which still looked sad. "Son, Miller," he said slowly, "I'm sorry. I guess I get a bad idea every now and then. This was a dilly. What in hell did I think I was about?"

Out of the corner of my eye I saw Guy Belcher stooping to retrieve the one hundred dollar bill. I still had a hard time believing something that small could pack that much wallop.

"I guess maybe now's not the time to tell him there's such a thing as a thousand dollar bill and that there's even a few ten thousand dollar bills in circulation," Guy Belcher said. He smiled. His teeth had yellow stains.

Turner didn't say a word. He looped one arm under my legs, one around my shoulders, and stood, holding me against him like I was a kid.

For the first time in a while I felt like a kid. It could've been worse.

Chapter Nine

I discovered I was tremendously hungry. Entangled in my love affair as I'd been and presently was, I'd forgotten or ignored hunger, had eaten nothing today save some oatmeal and toast early in the morning; now, guts rumbling but feeling good, grateful for the lean feel of my stomach, its hardness from a million sit-ups, hanging leg raises and sidebends, I found hunger lent a sharp edge to my desire. I wished now I'd brought my fifty-pound solid iron dumbbell along so I could do curls until my biceps were numb and swollen, then switch to one-arm military presses, then behind the neck triceps presses with both arms, anything to diminish that uncomfortable yet appealing effervescence tickling my groin.

After all, Yvonne (My lover!) was nearby and loving was surely in my near future.

Ordinarily, I'd have had a good upper body workout on Saturday afternoon, lots of chin-ups from the bar I'd fixed up in our attic, and maybe I'd see what I could do in the military press, then do set after set of dips between the wooden parallel bars I'd cobbled together from inch and a half dowels fitted through holes bored in two-by-four uprights. By then, I'd be drenched with sweat, "pumped," as bodybuilders say. Then, as my breathing slowed, I'd be filled with a wonderful after-orgasm-like lassitude that might last for up to an hour.

I pulled on jeans, tennis shoes over bare feet, a hooded sweatshirt, and headed out.

The shadows were lengthening. The longed-for dusk, which meant Yvonne, was imminent. My fingertips tingled. I wondered why Yvonne seemed fascinated with my hands, whose fingers were stubby and strong, covered with blond hairs she'd assured me "curved like golden scimitars . . ."

Except for our working time and the wedding, I'd hardly seen

Rex this weekend so I decided to stop by his cabin. Besides, I was curious to see how he was getting on with Christy.

A duckboard walkway led to his cabin door, and I'd just mounted it when the screen door, perhaps fifteen feet away, slammed back against the side of the cabin, and out came Donnie Redpath, clearly enraged, the nostrils of his blade-thin nose flaring like gills. Donnie stopped dead when he spotted me, surely one of his most hated objects on the Champs. I looked at him, hoping I was devoid of expression, and began to open and close my fists: this might be just what I needed, an opportunity to take this snotty arrogant prick of a frat-rat and boot his ass around a little.

He eyed me up and down, but I could see he was deciding against tangling with me.

I moved slowly toward him, and he stepped off the duckboards—a little like a scene in *Underground Man*—as I stalked slowly past him rather like a bristling dog.

At Rex's door I turned at a racket on the drive behind me—whipping around the drive came Jack Tudd, driving Donnie's jaunty yellow MG, its parking lights gleaming in the oncoming night. He came to an abrupt stop, pulled on the emergency brake and slid into the passenger's seat, leaving the driver's door open. Donnie strode toward the car and, without a word, got in and slammed the door.

As they sat there, engine idling throatily, Jack handed Donnie a bottle of Schlitz and Donnie lifted it to his lips and drank. When it was empty, he lowered the bottle, gave me a scathing look, wiped his mouth with the back of his long-boned hand, put the car in gear and accelerated out the circular drive—probably he and goofy Tudd were headed for the Torch Rivera at Silver Bridge three miles away for more beer. I heard the tires squeal several times as the MG hurtled toward the mouth of the resort, winding up tight in each gear.

I knocked lightly on Rex's door—three times, our signal. In seconds a smiling Rex in jeans, sweatsocks and T-shirt opened the door. I could see Christy behind him, sitting on the bed, wearing Rex's white shirt and a pair of Levi's cut-offs. When I came in she swung her legs around so her bare feet were on the rag rug by the bed. She looked pleased at my appearance, as if she welcomed a little novelty before she and Rex got back to what they'd been about: "Hi, Miller . . ." Her face was pinkish and a bit mottled, as if she'd wept and then dried her face and eyes and was now feeling much better, thank you. In fact, they both had the flushed and slightly disheveled look of a couple who'd been doing some serious making out. A sprig of Rex's black hair stuck up in the back like the blade of a knife. There were two half-eaten pieces of wedding cake on paper plates and two plastic forks on the dresser.

"Hi . . ."

"Christy here was just telling me she saw you had your eye on Lindsay Noel at the doings . . . what's that all about?" Rex asked.

"Yeah?"

"Yeah."

"I was telling Christy about last year—'member I told you about when I was janitorin' last year when she was in Ermine Falls School for the first two weeks and then pulled out to go live with her aunt in Ann Arbor and go to school there?"

"Yeah, I remembered her today when I saw her . . ."

"Yeah? Hell, Miller, I helped her out back then, and you're my brother, right, so she'd probably look kindly on you if you was to make a move . . . Christy here thinks you two'd make a nice-lookin' couple, Lindsay is I reckon about sweet sixteen, wouldn't you say, Christy?"

"Why, I'd have to say that's *exactly* what she is, Rex," Christy offered, grinning widely at my discomfiture. I noticed for the first time that, like Chaucer's Wife of Bath, she had an appealing gap between her front teeth.

"Really, Miller, I bet you could just go right up to her and just say"—she lowered her voice as she impersonated me—'Why, hi there, Lindsay, remember me? I'm Miller Springstead, Rex's brother.' 'Cause I just happen to know she thinks you're cute . . ."

Cute! F'Chrissakes! "Can't say's I probably ever spoke more than two words to her . . ."

"So much the better, Miller," Christy said, really enjoying herself now. "You won't have said anything to alienate her—you'll be starting with a clean slate, so to speak . . ."

"Not having to make no apologies in the beginning can definitely be an advantage," Rex added helpfully, grinning like a shark, enjoying this as much as Christy. Something had clearly passed between them since I'd eavesdropped on them in the cooler. Rex wet a finger and smoothed down that blade of hair at the back of his head. Then he sat down on the bed next to Christy.

Christy added: "*She* remembers *you*. Said she couldn't remember *ever* having said a word to you, either, but that she thought you were *cute* . . . cuter now than you were then . . . she wondered where you were, if you were going to be around . . . so what do you think, are you going to make it a point to be around? Where she is or might be, later this evening, I mean?"

"I dunno . . . where's she likely to be?" As soon as the question was uttered I felt as if I were betraying Yvonne.

The shift from Lindsay back to Yvonne reminded me I had to figure out where Yvonne was. Then I knew: *If you look along the shore there to the point . . . lift your eyes up so you can sort of see . . . promontory . . . lip of the bank kind of curls over . . . grove of cedars . . . crawl back into the inner part where there's a sort of little circle . . . cathedral feeling inside . . . trees leaning in sort of protectively . . .*

"Well," Christy said coyly, pressing her bare foot on Rex's ankle, "she's staying over at Bonnie Brae. Rex and I are going over there later, maybe you could just sort of drop in and see what happens, maybe we'll all end up on some sort of double date or something . . ."

Rex's face became pacific as a stroked spaniel's as Christy inched her foot further up under the cuff of his jeans, massaging his calf with her toes; then she brought her foot slowly down, catching the top of his sweatsock in her toes and pulling it down until it dangled from his instep.

"Well, okay," I said, "thanks for the tip," and got up to leave.

Neither tried to stop me and Rex had his arm around Christy's shoulders before I got out the door.

* * *

As I got closer, I thought I saw a figure seated out on the promontory's lip.

It occurred to me that were Yvonne to pitch forward, she'd roll down the steep embankment for fifty feet or so, then tumble into the chill water of Lake Albion.

Yvonne wore dark sneakers, her Levi's with the rolled cuffs and a huge black hooded sweatshirt rather like mine—no wonder she'd been so hard to see.

"It's a lovely place here," she said as I came up.

"Yeah . . . we dump leaves sometimes over the bluff . . ."

"I know. I think I'll speak to Ma and get her to put a bug in Renfrew's ear to do other than dump the goddamn things like that . . . so come closer, Miller Springstead, and as F. Scott Fitzgerald said in his notebook excerpts, later collected in *The Crack-Up* which was edited by Edmund Wilson, 'Draw your chair up to the edge of the precipice and I'll tell you a story'—no, just kidding, come on," she said, getting up. "Let's go hide in my little cubby, shall we . . . which for some reason this makes me recall a tiny poem of Antonio Machado's in its entirety: 'In the sea called woman, few men shipwreck at night; many at sunrise' . . ."

"Sure. So what's the story you're fixing to tell me?"

"Not really *tell*, my dear, *write*: and *we're* the story, you and I, the story I hope I'm going to write some day, though of course, we'll both be so cleverly disguised only you and I will know who we really are . . . and, of course, as art it may all come to nothing, as such things often do. As someone once said, 'the waste basket is the writer's best friend' . . ."

"So tell me the story . . ."

"Well. I can't. Yet. I haven't written it. Yet. I won't know what it's really going to be until I try to do it—it's not like writing an essay where you start with a conclusion. With this kind of thing you sort of figure out what you're doing in the act of doing it . . . hmmm, p'raps there's a certain analogy to our, uh, relationship, do you suppose? Fitzgerald—and I guess I have him on the brain tonight—once said there were only two basic stories, 'Jack and the Beanstalk' and 'Cinderella'—quest stories or personal transformation stories, though of course they're just different sides of the same coin . . . which do you think *our* story might bear the most resemblance to?"

"God, more riddles," I said, feeling all this classy literary chatter fluttering over my head. However, in such cases, I always tried to respond honestly: "How would I know? Until I read Chekhov I thought O. Henry was the greatest story writer ever and Poe was next. Can't you just sort of tell me what you think our story's *maybe* going to be about, or what sort of happens in it? Then I can answer you . . ."

"Well. You're smarter than you look—just kidding"—she reached out and tweaked my nose— "for God's sake, don't get that, that *glowery* look. So okay, seriously then, I guess I intend for it to be a kind of love story, not necessarily tragic, but sort of . . . *bittersweet*, shall we say, maybe a little in spirit like 'The Lady With the Pet Dog' . . . but it'll be about an older woman and a younger man. They connect for various reasons of chemistry, circumstance and perceived affinity, at least on the part of the woman . . . of *course* she finds him toothsome . . . p'raps it's a bit otherwise with the male lead, because he's mostly fueled by the novelty of it all and the simple desire of youth, which God knows can be a lovely thing, and which perhaps provides some of the lovely excitement of the sort that's been missing from her life for far, far too long . . . I don't really know too much yet, I'll have to discover it as I write, but I think I know that when their honeyed hours end, they'll still try to meet when they can, as much as their circumstances and ingenuity permit. Which may not be often, but often enough to sustain them, at least for a while, until . . ."

"Until what?"

"The inevitable. He ages, as does she, and at some point it's in*ev*itable that she'll truly become more 'older woman' than 'lover' and his eye will in*ev*itably fall upon someone his own age and, well, guess how it turns out? Does it sound sad? No matter, it's all inevitable, and as I say, I mean for the outcome to be bittersweet, though I suppose that's a loaded word. You're a bright young man, Miller, and you can probably guess the larger outlines of what the future holds for us. But to bring the focus back to us as we are at this precise moment, Miller, I can tell you this about the future: for the moment, it doesn't matter. As in 'The Lady With the Pet Dog,' all that *really* matters is that the end is somewhere in the future, that it's not *now* . . . oh, and I think I've got at least a working title: *This Sweetest Day*. Sound syrupy? Glutinous? Sentimental? Guess it is. Well, I'll use another title but keep the line from Keats for the epigraph: 'This sweetest day for dalliance was born!' You like?"

Yes, I liked. I demonstrated how much by pulling her to me, pressing us together until we both could hardly breathe, and I didn't think a bit about Lindsay Noel in the crush.

"I was afraid—only momentarily, of course—that you mightn't divine where I was going to be tonight," she said when we parted for air. "I'd have been awfully put out if you hadn't remembered what I'd said on the dock last night because that would have meant I'd misread something about you and . . . I'm not sure the story I plan to write would have worked out the way I wanted it to if that'd been the case—though of course that's the wonderful thing about fiction, it's a fluid and plastic medium, unlike, say, memoir . . . but I'm digressing, aren't I, see the effect you have on me? Come a little closer . . . say, I bet you have something I don't . . ."

"Yeah, I *do* have something I know you don't," I said, aware of the arrowhead in my pocket—I could feel its sharp point pressing into my thigh. "But I'll fix that up in a minute."

"Perhaps we're talking about two different things—what I really don't have at the moment is underwear."

"Really?"

"Really. Would you like me to demonstrate? Or would you prefer to find out for yourself? But whatever were *you* talking about?"

"This." I put the naked arrowhead into her palm, wondering if I ought to have wrapped it in something appropriate, say a piece of deerskin. "I've found half a dozen over the years, but this's the prettiest and best executed one . . . I noticed you're wearing a gold chain without anything on it and I thought you might get a jeweler to fix it so you could hang the arrowhead from it . . ." It thrilled me to imagine the point of sharp flint dangling hidden between her breasts.

"Why it's perfectly *beautiful*, Miller. What a wonderful example of flaking. Nineteenth century Ojibway, no doubt. It's almost beautiful enough to make me tell you I love you for giving it to me, but that wouldn't be productive and so I most assuredly won't. Thank you, my dear. I'll cherish and treasure this. Now come along. So I can show you what I don't have."

She pulled me by the hand over to the cedar grove and knelt down to show me the passageway leading into the grove's cubby.

On her hands and knees before me, Yvonne began to crawl through the portal; I dropped to my knees and crawled after her, her rounded denim-clad behind swaying before me as she wriggled forward. About eight feet in the passageway through the closely ranked cedars debouched into a sort of hollowed out circular chamber, and there on ground, covered with cedar boughs turned brown but still springy and shining faintly from starshine filtering through cracks in the dome, were two identical, rolled blue sleeping bags.

Yvonne sat back on the heels of her sneakers and untied the drawstring of a sleeping bag and began to unroll it as I crawled over to her. I did likewise with the other. It was made of nylon and its cool slickness against my fingertips reminded me of sex. Of course, lately just about everything did.

The bower's ceiling was no more than a foot above our heads as we faced each other, both of us on our knees and sitting back on our heels, the down-filled nylon bags lolling out before us like puffy blue tongues. Then Yvonne made a few hobbling steps toward me on her knees and we were close enough to kiss.

* * *

The continuous touch of the bouffant nylon, slick as a cool puddle of oil below us, added to our tactile excitement: at one point, Yvonne rolled me over on my back—easy enough since under her touch I'd no more volition than a Raggedy Andy.

"See how you like this, my darling . . . you can tell me later . . ."

The experience of her mouth, teeth and tongue took me beyond anything I'd called ecstasy: what I'd previously thought of as ultimate was merely as foothills were to mountains.

Later she asked: "Did you like that?"

"Any part of you touching me or me touching you is always pleasurable . . . maybe some day I'll be able to believe all this . . ."

"Aren't you sweet. You know, you're doing very nicely in the area of sensual appreciation, Miller, you're coming to grasp something many, many men never do, that for a woman it's the process more than the conclusion that matters most, though that's not to discount the utter thrill of the 'little death,' as the French say. I know I said earlier I didn't believe in obligatory gifts, but lovers' acts may be another matter . . ."

"Yes."

"Oh good. My darling lover who brings me the 'little death' and lovely arrowheads and many other things I cherish. Come here, lover, and please think kindly of me in the years to come . . ."

I cast my eyes briefly heavenward. Through gaps in the cedars I could see, faintly, bits of the insensible constellations wheeling through the night sky, and knew that the new moon was close, cloaked though it presently was, waiting to wax forth from the first sickle-shaped fleck of brilliance finally into a full hunter's moon: surely it would begin tomorrow.

Turkeys

August 1952

It had been Rex's turn for morning milking, but I'd done it because Rex had gone down early to the MacReady's to help Sonney patch his barn roof. When I was done, I went to the barnyard gate and opened it for Elizabeth and watched her amble off with that sloppy walk cows have. Once through the gate, she usually headed for a spot over by the southwest corner of the pasture where there was an artesian well and water trickled slowly but continuously from a corroded pipe. The grass was always bright green around it. It took a couple of minutes to fill a gallon jug from it as we sometimes did since it had a clear, slightly sweet taste and Turner swore by it as a thirst-quencher.

It was the kind of summer day Turner liked: not too hot, not too cold, just the right amount of breeze, plenty of sun, blue sky and fat white clouds zipping around.

I shut the gate and walked toward the house, figuring to have some Wheaties, milk and orange juice, but about halfway to the door I heard a diesel engine idling down by the shop.

Curious, I turned left and walked toward the shop, which was set back maybe fifty feet off Michigan 115. It was just what I thought, a parked semi—and I recognized it. Two weeks ago the driver, a guy named Jack, had made arrangements for Turner to rebuild a transmission for the C-20 Chevy pickup he had back in Georgia; he'd planned to pick it up and take it back with him in the semi on his next swing through. Jack was a skinny gink with long, greasy gray hair, long sideburns and shiny bald spot. He wore the usual greasy, green twill trousers and shirt most drivers wore, with a namepatch over his right pocket.

When I was almost to the shop, I turned and looked over at the semi. Instead of the usual covered trailer, this one looked like a kind of prison on wheels except that, instead of vertical bars, its sides were entirely covered with steel mesh.

I changed direction and headed over to the idling truck, curious.

When I got closer, I saw why he'd parked it next to a decent-sized maple—it was filled from top to bottom and end to end with cages filled with young turkeys. A powerful smell of shit, sickness and rotted hay swept over me. Jack had parked his semi where it was out of the sun and caught a bit of breeze.

It was a huge honeycomb of cages and it was hard to believe so many turkeys could be packed in that little a space: three or sometimes four birds were crammed in cages not much bigger than a three-foot cube. There must have been hundreds of them, tier upon tier of the stinking, suffering ugly birds. On the bottom three tiers were the dead, the half-dead and the dying. For some reason, I remembered when Rex and I had stayed with the MacReadys during the war. I'd go out to the privy and see, down through the hole, a multi-colored, cone-shaped mountain of shit daily rising toward me, and as I put my ass on the worn wood hole, I always half-feared a shit-monster was going to poke thick turd fingers up through the hole and grab me by the pecker and pull me right down through the hole and down on top of him, where I'd sink into him and be digested alive.

As I got closer, many sets of stupid turkey eyes focussed bleakly upon me. Their scaly legs and ugly feet protruded through the gaps in the cages, their shit and its scent was everywhere. Then I suddenly realized that the biggest and strongest had been put on the uppermost tiers and had shit down on the smaller ones below, where they weakened and died. Maybe Jack stopped every now and then to shift them around.

Sickened, I turned away from the sad birds who had, all the time I'd stood there, made not a sound, just looked at me. I double-timed it back to the house, feeling eyes on my back.

* * *

I made lunch and at noon Turner listened to five minutes of news from CBS in New York on his Sky Buddy as he sipped a big glass of iced coffee and sugar and milk. Then he began to slowly eat his baloney and mayonnaise and lettuce and cheese sandwich; I'd made one for him and one for me.

I could see he was thinking over the radio news, making me wonder again why he was so damned interested because it seemed to me there wasn't much he, me nor anybody else, except maybe politicians and the armed forces, could do about most things—except hear about how whatever had already happened had already happened. Lately, he'd been wrapped up in some stuff revolving around a Negro convict named Heywood Patterson who'd died of cancer at age thirty-eight in Jackson Prison and who'd been one of the nine "Scottsboro Boys" who were supposed to have raped a woman—except that they didn't, some claimed.

"You ain't hungry?" he asked, finally focussing on me, his eyes somewhat losing that far away look. "How come?"

"When that guy from Georgia was in the shop, I went over to his rig and looked his load of turkeys over . . . what a stink, kinda took away my appetite, I guess . . ."

Turner pushed his own, half-eaten sandwich away. "Mine too," he said shortly, as if he wished I'd never brought the subject up.

"You seen 'em?"

"From a distance . . . didn't need to go closer. By now I know pretty much what I'm going to see with turkeys, or any livestock, for that matter . . ."

"How come they pack them in like that?"

"Money," Turner said curtly. "Probably the truck company took their cue from how they used to load ships with African slaves and bring 'em over here to pick our cotton and change our sheets and empty our thundermugs."

"Well, *I* sure won't eat none anymore—I'd be damned if I'm gonna pay for any as gets treated like that . . ."

"You haven't had to pay for nothing so far, pal, at least where money's concerned," Turner said, but the sharp edge was gone from his voice. "Listen, Miller, men do the same damn things to men as you seen 'em do with them sad-ass turkeys. Jack there, he's not a bad guy, you seen how he parked in the shade where there was a breeze. What you probably don't know is how he does his best to keep 'em watered, and how he'll pull off the road and clean out the shit and the dead ones to give the others a little more space.

"Y'know, Miller, in the military I once had brig duty for a couple of weeks, and I don't mean no cobbled-together detention place made out of an old storeroom, but a real brig with cell blocks that housed two thousand men. You know what a cell block is? I didn't until then, but it's a damned accurate term and what it is ain't too far off from how them turkeys was accommodated, the main exception being that in a human cell block the prisoners didn't shit on one another's heads. Anyhow, that's what it was, a fucking *cell block*: in this big room you'd have a big square block—of cells! Three tiers up, basically cages with three walls but without holes in the floor to shit through like the turkeys. There'd be two or three men to a cage, awaiting their fate just like the poor damn turkeys, except they more or less knew what was coming and most figured they'd get through it and know freedom yet, and that kept 'em going. You see that sandwich there you're feeling too shitty to eat? Where you reckon that comes from? I'll tell you: from hog snouts and feet and jowls and bellies and innards and crap ain't good enough for other things, and when I go buy that sonofabitching package of lunch meat down to Guilder's, I'm paying a penny or two to the people that cut the hogs' throats."

"How can you eat it knowing all that?"

"How can you not? A man's got to live, just like the critters that eat other critters straight out without going through what we do. But how you deal with it all is a real good question. And I clearly ain't got the answer. Anyhow, what I do is, I just try to take things in a bit at a time, y'know, so's not to let it all sink in at once: who could take on all them things at once, the death camps in the ETO, then things I personally seen in the South Pacific. And slaughterhouses. Whorehouses. Orphanages. Nut wards. I tell you, Miller, I think if I thought hard about all the critters that have to die just today all around the globe for our food and gloves and grease and other crap, if I ever let all that cave in on me at once, I'd expect to go off like a Roman candle . . ."

It was a long speech for Turner and I was left speechless.

Turner got up abruptly, one hand squeezing the other as if he were shaking hands with himself, the muscles of his arms twisting like snakes. "Nevertheless," he said, seeming to direct himself toward some invisible person standing behind me, "we don't need to eat any more turkey if you don't want to, not even Thanksgiving or Christmas . . ."

But what if I start to think about it all and then I find I can't stop and the dam busts and it all just rolls over me? I wanted to ask.

"Thanks," I said.

Chapter Ten

As agreed upon the night before as we left her bower, Yvonne and I met on the help dock for a swim Sunday morning at 6:30. This was surely the last such we'd share for some time, maybe, it occurred to me, forever. What would our time together be called by either of us a decade hence? An episode? Maybe in her case, a story?

We didn't speak, barely nodded, but we came naturally to stand side-by-side in the chill morning gloom, our shoulders almost but not quite touching, looking at the dark, faintly corrugated water of Lake Albion. Yvonne was again swaddled in her heavy dark robe, which made her look small on this morning, while I again wore my hooded sweatshirt and the oyster-colored sweatpants over trunks. We'd both brought beach towels—I'd slipped into Rex's cabin and borrowed his, sure he wouldn't mind.

We stood motionless. I was on edge to rip off my sweatclothes and make the plunge but waited for her to initiate things.

I looked over at Yvonne. She was biting her lips and trembling. Her eyes were shut tight but leaked no tears.

Finally, I touched her hand lightly, turned and pulled my sweatshirt over my head. She let her robe fall into a soft heap at her feet. She wore a black tank suit, and though I felt the inappropriateness of it for this rather somber goodbye swim, I could not stop myself from imagining what it would be like to peel it from her as I might the skin from a delectable fruit.

* * *

(The swim itself: again the lake's heart-stopping cold. Our faces are inches apart as we gasp from the cold and, treading water, look into each other's faces, then swim toward separate ends of the dock, then come back, criss-crossing twice. After probably no more than a minute immersed we clamber up on the dock. Yvonne, trembling, lower lip clamped in her teeth, retrieves and struggles into her robe without a glance at me. Then she gives me a brief look: her face is anguished and glistens with water or tears or both in the early morning light.)

(As she mounts the wooden stairs leading up and past the pavilion and I stand, dumbly watching—shivering, my heart contracts as I accept what Yvonne has reminded me from the start, that this moment has always been inevitable—I think of Anna Sergeyevna in "The Lady With the Pet Dog," and how at the prospect of parting from Gurov "she was not crying but was so sad that she seemed ill, and her face was quivering.")

* * *

I was almost to my cabin before I became aware of HG's brown Ford station wagon parked behind it almost exactly where Yvonne and I had waxed her Chevy yesterday morning, its driver's side door slightly ajar. I didn't see HG anywhere about so continued on to my cabin door. My hand had closed on the screen door knob when I heard a sound from the station wagon.

HG had apparently been lying supine on the front seat on his back, and when he pushed the driver's door further open, his head lolled down from the seat until he was looking upside down into the colorful leaves of the maple near the cabin. In a moment he laboriously hoisted himself up, using the steering wheel to get himself into a seated position. He looked over at me: "*Whah-hah-hah*," went his breathy chortle-laugh. "Whew, what a way to get your circulation going, eh, Miller, makes a fella dizzy, whah-hah-hah . . ."

HG swung himself around so he faced me and put his feet—in loafers with no socks—on the ground before him. From the car seat he plucked up his small curved silver flask and extended it to me. I faked a sip and put it back into his shaking left hand.

"Here's where my affinity with Lowry shows, Miller, in my

intense identification with his poem 'He Liked the Dead': 'The grass was not green not even grass to him; nor was the sun, sun; rose, rose; smoke, smoke; limb, limb'; or how about 'Prayer for Drunks' in its entirety: 'God give those drunkards drink who wake at dawn, Gibbering on Beelzebub's bosum, all outworn, As once more through the windows they espy, Looming, the dreadful Pontefract of day.' The end. Whew. Know what Pontefract is, Miller? It's a pile of medieval ruins in merry old England . . . Pomfret Castle in Shakespeare . . . ah, Lowry, old Lowry, who just this past year chased thirty sodium amytal pills with a quart of gin and strangled to death on his vomit—Death by Misadventure, the coroner called it, Miller! Think of it! Death by Misadventure—now there's a term with . . . with *balls*, whah-hah-hah . . . how's about this: 'And the cries, which might be the groans of the dying, Or the groans of love.' Top flight!

"So long, then, Miller," he said, slowly, as if he were in pain, swinging his legs around and placing his feet on the pedals. "Good luck with trying to be a writer, Miller—and oh, if you'll forgive me one last quote: 'Over the town, in the dark tempestuous night, backwards revolved the luminous wheel.' Last line of Chapter One of *Under the Volcano*. And here's another for you to remember, Miller, this's the passage from Roethke's 'Four for Sir John Davies' that was to've been the epigraph for my fabulous novel *Clumsy Partners*—I should say *is* because the typescript, the copyedited typescript, is ready to go to the typesetter, is still extant, unbeknownst of course to my lovely and beguiling Yvonne, we guys gotta keep a *few* secrets, n'est-ce pas, but that's all it is, that's what I've come to embody: inert typescript, unless, of course, through some fluke of fate it, as they say, ultimately 'Sees the Light,' as they say, if you know what I mean and I'm sure you do . . . and if you don't you will . . . *whah-hah-hah* . . . so get a listen at this: 'I know a dance the elephants believe. The living all assemble, what's the cue? Do what the clumsy partner wants to do!' You see, Miller, I got m'*magnum opus* right here beside me, my l'il pard, he's kinda riding shotgun for me today, you might say . . ." On the floor mat of the passenger's side I saw a gray manuscript box with its top off. The first page was the title page, and there were red marks on some of the typed lines. "So, so long, Miller, so long, me'n *Clumsy Partners* gotta continue our odyssey . . . so long, so long . . . don't take any wooden nickels . . ."

HG's knuckles turned white as he gripped the steering wheel with one hand and started the engine with the other; the powerful V-8 throbbed to life and the wagon shook. The door creaked part-way shut, then slammed, and I watched Professor Harrison Goode pull slowly away, filling me with profound relief and a new sense of sympathy for Yvonne: Christ, what would it be like to live around a guy like that, day in and day out, if in five minutes he wore you out and made you want to be anywhere but in his presence?

* * *

I decided to drop by Rex's cabin to see what was up with him and when he wanted to go home. My timing was perfect, because I came upon a scene: Donnie Redpath stood on the wooden walkway to Rex's cabin, his face tomato-red with something—rage, shame, humiliation, maybe all three, it was hard to tell—as he confronted Rex and Christy, who'd just stepped from the cabin door and stood on the walkway perhaps a dozen feet from Donnie. Christy wore Rex's heavy dark-green flannel shirt. Her thighs were bare but she didn't look cold; she looked flushed and angry.

Rex stood beside and slightly behind her, shirtless and shoeless, wearing jeans. He had a rather bemused look as he regarded Donnie—"Try this on for size, you college dipshit, here you came here looking to score and guess what, prick, I aced you out—"

Donnie's MG idled on the drive behind him, and as I watched, Jack Tudd got out of the passenger's side—it took a while for him to maneuver his bulk out of the tiny compartment. Finally he stood ponderously, lifting his hand to shade his eyes as he like me assessed things.

"I'm not *your* girl!" Christy angrily answered what had apparently been a question or assertion from Donnie. She left Rex's side and took a step closer to him, her small fists balling: "I was *never* your girl, there's no *way* I would *ever* be your girl, and I don't know who the hell you think you are coming up here and thinking you got some kind of *claim* on me—well, you *don't*, so just stuff *that* up your pipe and smoke it!"

"I can't believe this shit! You and this swamprat! This dumbbell with three pounds of gristle for brains! I drove *six hundred fucking miles* to be here with you!"

The easygoing grin left Rex's face when he heard the words dumbbell, gristle and swamprat, and now he began to shamble slowly forward toward Donnie, open hands hanging at his sides. I knew that sleepy, loose-limbed slouch well, had always felt it a kind of privilege to watch Rex explode into action from what seemed near-somnolence and stasis; he was awfully good in this sort of situation.

But Christy was after him in a flash, grabbing his arm, then, when that failed, pulling him back by the waistband of his jeans: "No, Rex *please*, don't you *dare*, can't you see he's not *worth* it?" She had a solid grip on him and she planted her bare feet firmly, the better to restrain him. I liked her considerably at that moment.

Donnie'd seen me and shifted his attention my way: here was the guy who'd manhandled him when he was in his cups Friday night, and shamed him before his aunt Yvonne as well.

I smiled at him, waiting for him to decide what to do.

Hey, here came a new wrinkle: out of the corner of my eye I saw Jack Tudd, who after getting out of Donnie's MG and surveying things had slyly sidled around to the periphery of events and begun to lumber in our direction, his fat thighs brushing until he was running awkwardly at Rex's blind side, arms extended to send Rex sprawling and salvage the pride of his mentor and hero, Great Donnie Redpath.

Rex must have noticed him about the same time I did. He didn't even have to free himself from Christy's restraining grip to quickly step back a pace and in a classic maneuver stick out his foot and trip the barreling Tudd so he flew over the wooden walkway in a kind of truncated swan dive and landed in the dirt about three feet from the left side of Rex's front door. He looked up to orient himself and spat out dirt, grass and part of a large brown maple leaf.

Rex and I both laughed aloud, coarsely, mockingly, then Rex turned abruptly and followed Christy back into his cabin, while I just as abruptly turned east and headed back toward my cabin, leaving Donnie to help—presumably—his pal up. I hoped he did, but didn't look back for confirmation. I recalled hearing Donnie at Friday's buffet supper say in a joking voice to his pal and "Brother Delt," "You annoying bastard, Tudd, whyn't ya go move your bowels or something else that'll keepya out of the picture for half an hour . . ."

I'd almost reached my own cabin when I heard the MG tearing away at top speed, winding up tight in each gear as it fled the Champs.

Suddenly I felt tired of them all, Harrison Goode, Rex, Christy, Donnie, Tudd, Yvonne, Duane, Ardis, even the bride and groom themselves, the whole kit and kaboodle. I thought with sudden longing of our raggedy orchard at home high up on the hill above our home and junkyard where we'd always buried our pets and where I'd found Yvonne's arrowhead. I resolved to go up there and take a look around as soon as I got back. For now, though, I'd do the next best thing—go in my cabin, get under the covers and take a nap. I was still starving but didn't feel like eating.

I was a few yards away from my cabin door when I heard the MG coming back in low gear, making another circle of the Champs' drive; then, from over by the kitchen Donnie's parting howl of rage rose above the clatter of his MG: "*Sonsabitches! I hate you all! I hope you all fucking die! Yai-eeeeee! Yai-eeeeee!*"

* * *

I awakened to find Yvonne in dark stockings, a dark knee-length skirt and a turquoise sweater over a madras blouse, looking somberly down on me. The color of her sweater made her eyes dark green and she again looked sad almost to the point of illness, again like Anna in Chekhov's story. She cast her gaze around the cabin as if committing its details to memory: for use in her story-to-be?

"Uh, hi," I managed, getting awkwardly out from under the covers and standing in T-shirt and oyster sweatpants. She stepped into my arms and we hugged each other for long seconds—rather chastely at first, then I could feel her relax into me and I put my hand on her resilient bottom, feeling the lovely cleft of her ass beneath my fingertips.

"Sorry if I seem distracted, Miller, I've been looking for HG, I haven't seen him since yesterday and I'm getting worried, I have no *idea* what kind of mischief or jam he might have gotten himself into . . . or if he's in jail or if maybe he just went off to the Fox Haus in Traverse where he sometimes likes to stay and is under an assumed name trying to get himself in condition to drive back to St. Louis . . ."

"Christ, he was here earlier, Yvonne, talking to me, what's it now, about 11:00? Hell, he must have been here around 7:00 this morning, he turned up by my cabin when I came back from swimming with you . . . and then he drove off in his wagon . . . didn't look half bad, a little shaky, maybe . . ."

Maybe I should have kept my stupid mouth shut, I thought, my hand still warming against her wool-clad ass—the last thing I wanted to think about—or have her think about—was her fucked up husband and his plight.

"Don't worry about HG," I said, "he was going on about his novel, but otherwise looked more or less okay . . ."

Yvonne went taut and put her hand behind her back and pulled my hand away from her ass; it was not a lovely moment.

"His novel?"

"Well, yeah, he had it lying beside him on the floormat, big bunch of typed sheets in a box . . . what's the problem?"

A stricken look had overtaken her face, as if she'd just heard an unbearably sad tale of some appealing creature horribly mangled by a speeding car.

"Oh, God," she moaned and her lower lip began to tremble. Her eyes took on a glassy sheen. "Miller, you've *got* to help me find him . . ."

"Sure, okay, but he's probably already out on I-75 by now . . ."

"No! He's *here*, on the Champs . . . I know, I can *feel* it . . ."

"Looked to me like he was ready to beat it on out of here for good . . ."

"Oh, yes," she said, her mouth suddenly turning down in that hard-boiled way she occasionally affected, "figuratively that's no doubt true . . . which is why he's close by . . . does that sound like a paradox to you?"

"I don't understand . . ."

Yvonne looked at me angrily: "Because he's got that stupid *manuscript* with him. Because he'd *never* go away to do anything dreadful but would do it right in front of us, he'd want to rub our *noses* in his despair—and he'd hope at least to make us acknowledge our part in it—but it's *his* goddamn fault, not mine . . . nor Mom's nor his sister's nor Daphne's any more than it's *your* fault! You tell me, you know this place as well as I do: where would he go, where could he hide himself and that stupid, hideous, overpowered shit-colored station wagon, that turd on wheels, where he and it wouldn't be found until it was way, way too late? Oh, God, this is just *like* him . . ."

This Dumbbell

July 1956

I can hear Turner moving slowly up the narrow staircase to the attic Rex and I occupy and I feel myself get alert.

Turner hardly ever comes up here, believing each of us, including himself, should have a good bit of privacy.

I sit on the bench press bench I made last week out of two-by-fours and two-by-sixes, listening. I'm not much of a carpenter like Rex is and like Turner can be, though Turner dislikes working with wood, preferring metal, but still I took my time and it's sturdy and looks pretty good, not that that's anybody's concern. Two two-by-sixes make the bench part that I lie on when pressing the barbell (180's presently on the bar); doubled two-by-fours make the front legs and the back legs, which continue on into uprights with V's cut in them, with sheet metal screwed to the V's to make the crutch where the bar rests. I covered the bench with inch-thick foam rubber from a wreck in the yard, then covered that with burlap materials from some seat covers, also from the yard, securing the burlap to the wood with Turner's staple gun.

I figure Turner, who's not seen my bench, may be coming up to check it out. Then, as he appears at the top of the staircase, I notice he's moving slowly and seems to be listing to the right, and for half a second I feel a pang of fear that he's drunk—though why I should think that I don't know, since as far as I know he's not drunk anything since he's been back from the war; and I was so young when he went overseas I can remember hardly anything of him or what he did or didn't do before he left.

Now I see why he's pulling to the right—he's carrying a solid dumbbell, two big iron balls on either end of a short steel bar.

Turner's in his green twill work clothes and he stands there holding the dumbbell, surveying the interior and letting his eyes adjust to the dimness. Then he focusses on me sitting on my bench in old swimming trunks and no shirt. He moves a little closer and checks out my bench from where he stands for a few seconds, still holding the dumbbell. His head moves slightly up and down, suggesting approval. He moves a little closer to the bench, stepping onto the old oval-shaped braided rag rug Pearl MacReady gave me that I've got my dumbbells sitting on. Turner's arm muscles swell as he sets the big dumbbell gently down on the rug.

"Bought this here fifty-pounder over at the East Jordan foundry for two bucks," he says. "Not bad, eh? Too bad there wasn't two. Some guy'd had it in with a bunch of scrap. Like to know its history. Anyhow, it ought to make you a pretty decent addition to your equipment . . ." He nods to me and heads back to the stairwell.

I'm still kind of stunned. "Pa!" I cry after him. "Thanks, Pa! She's a beauty. Thanks again!" Even before I touch it I know this will become an object I will want with me all my life.

* * *

The steel bar is cold as winter when my fingers close around it.

I bring the dumbbell over and put it on my bunk, where it sinks deeply into the mattress. There's a raised fifty on one end. The balls are rust-colored now, but I can see traces of the black paint they once wore. I touch the dumbbell here and there, examining it minutely, thrilled; for some reason I have always liked things that are used rather than new, and this has clearly been used. And has no moving parts, nothing to ever go wrong: it'll be as good in a thousand years or in ten thousand or a million as it is right now, unless it gets melted down for scrap as almost happened.

I sit on the edge of my bunk, take the dumbbell in my right hand, brace my elbow against the inside of my thigh, and do half a dozen curls, then do the same with my left hand. The flushing of my biceps with blood feels great, but far beyond the dumbbell's mere utility, I know I will keep it with me until I die. Nor will I forget the moment I watched Turner bend over and gently place the dumbbell on the rug.

I look over at the barbell resting on the bench's crutch—I bought a 110 pound barbell-dumbbell set when I was fourteen, but didn't have to buy any more plates for a while because Turner gave me two forty-five pound flywheels which he'd bored out in the shop and ground the teeth off of.

I sit there, one hand on each cold iron ball of my new-old dumbbell.

* * *

Finally a thought flits into my head like some kind of winged and barbed night insect: I touch the steel handle between the two iron spheres and it's still cold as ice: how long will this dumbbell be around, how long after the flesh has left my bones and the bones of those I love?

The disparity between flesh and iron makes me gasp. Where will it, and we, be in a thousand years? Ten thousand? A million?

A cool breeze enters from the partly open window at the far end of the attic, passes over my bare skin, and I shudder, remembering the first cold feel of the steel bar between the iron globes as my perishable hand closed around it.

Chapter Eleven

As we walked, Yvonne talked: "Now is the time when I have to be strong. I've always known this was coming, or something like it, God, these last three years of his *relentless* drinking have been just *waiting* for the other dreadful shoe to fall . . . and now what's been long-dreaded has come to me here and now, what do I *do*? I want so *much* to just be no longer *responsible*, Miller . . ."

"Why don't you just up and leave him?"

"Why? Oh, ho, ho, how little you know, my boy. Well, if you must know, it's because in spite of everything else, he makes extremely *won*derful coffee—grinds the beans himself and adds a little chicory—oh, don't look so *solemn*, Miller, I'm just teasing, for God's sake—if I weren't able to laugh at some of these things who knows where I'd be. Dead, probably. In fact, where am I? Oh, *God*, Miller, I'm still with HG for any number of reasons—look, you may have been raised hard-scrabble but you don't have an inkling of what the academic life can be like, its pressures and exigencies. Well, okay, here's why, too: I'm a woman, otherwise alone, and I don't *have* a whole lot of resources, just my modest trust fund and a teaching credential . . . and I've become accustomed to, as they say, the amenities of life . . . and if I left I'd lose my share of a considerable inheritance from HG's family that'll be along one of these times, and I love the *extremely* pleasant house we live in, and the area in which we live, and I like St. Louis. Why ask? What've you got to offer me besides certain momentary delights of the flesh? 'Come live with me and be my love?' God! Miller, imagine us, if you can, in some cramped little campus apartment, trying to live on love and bumping into each other and getting irritable. You know, Dr. Johnson said fish and guests both begin to stink after three days, and three days, the three days we've shared have been *lovely*, dear, but trying to *protract* our experiences would be *sheerest* folly, Miller. Listen to me, I know what I'm talking about!" She was by now weeping a bit as she walked and talked, though a quivering smile tried to impose itself on her lips from time to time. "Just *imagine* us in some tiny apartment, short on money, me putting you through school as my aging outpaced yours? Terrifying. One thing that doesn't scare me, though, is the prospect of solitude. Didn't Einstein say in 'Self-Portrait' that if solitude is painful in youth, in maturity it becomes delicious? And I'm not nearly as strong as you probably think I am, Miller. Not nearly . . . in fact, I'm not strong at all, no, not a bit . . ."

Feeling myself losing her second-by-second, I said, "I love you . . ." (I could hear a horselaugh from Rex in the back of my head.)

"Oh, God, don't *say* that, we agreed, didn't we? Lovers are what we really are, darling, and that should be enough. Didn't Camus say in one of his notebooks that all he knew of love was that it was this strange mixture of intelligence, affection and desire he felt for this or that person? Maybe we have that, but we certainly don't have what Fitzgerald in *Tender is the Night*—it's a lovely book, and you *must* read it someday—called 'a wild submergence of soul, a dipping of all colors into an obscuring dye' . . . probably a damned good thing, too, considering our ages and other differences . . ."

And with that she stopped, wiped her eyes with the back of her hand, smiled and kissed me with a different kind of kiss: it was on the lips, loving and predominately sad, yet without a hint we were—perhaps now it was had been—lovers. It was a kiss of benediction or farewell. Or both.

* * *

We'd walked perhaps a hundred yards along the drive toward the resort's entrance and the state road that took you toward the interstates and what was thought of as civilization; we stepped off the road and paused by a padlocked orange gasoline pump with a hand crank where, in years past, Rex and I had occasionally filled Turner's pickup when hauling leaves away or doing other Champs errands.

Yvonne and I looked at each other blankly, apparently realizing the same thing at the same time: that HG might be any of a hundred places, he might already be tooling his way to St. Louis on I-75 (my best guess), a bottle of cognac cradled in his crotch. He might be parked over beneath the chestnut tree by Bonnie Brae on the other side of the Champs, sleeping his excesses off. Or, as Yvonne had suggested, the Fox Haus in Traverse. Or he might be . . .

We seemed to hear it at the same time: a powerful engine somewhere nearby, idling. A V-8.

We turned toward the sound: directly across the road from us, set back into slightly rising ground amid a host of medium-sized maples, was an old two-car garage. Originally a stable, it had later been converted for cars, though it'd seldom been used in recent years. Painted barn red some years back and now well-faded, it blended so well into the turned leaves of the maples surrounding it on three sides that it was easy to walk or drive past and never remark it.

The idling got louder as we slowly approached the building, and by the time we reached the sliding doors I could distinctly hear the Ford wagon's noisy valve lifters.

At last something my strength was good for: I seized an edge of the door with both hands and heaved—it shot back, emitting a short metallic shriek, and I rammed it as far as it'd go, exposing about three-quarters of the ten foot doorway. A cloud of stinking light blue exhaust billowed out into the open air.

I took a deep breath, ran into the putrid and nauseating interior, exhaust stinging my eyes, and quickly found the station wagon's driver's side door. I jerked it open to find HG supine, stretched across the seat. With the door open, his head slipped over the end of the seat and lolled back, exposing a surprisingly thin throat—but in the quick glimpse I took, his face looked benign, as if he were finally getting that good night's sleep he probably hadn't had in years.

I reached across him for the friction-taped ignition switch, turned the motor off, then caught HG up under his arms and dragged him face up out of the car and back to the door and a couple of steps out into a thin heatless noontime sun that cast thin shadows. I laid him down on his back and staggered away to gulp fresh air. Then I turned back to him.

Yvonne stood flat-footed and horror-struck, immobilized, unable to help as I bent over her husband. I caught HG up under his armpits again and dragged him further away from the garage, whose interior was still exuding gray exhaust. He was heavier than I would have guessed and was lax as a just-killed animal, making an unwieldy burden. His heels kept catching on things and by the time I got him into the open he'd lost one wine-colored loafer. His sockless foot looked especially pitiful.

As Yvonne looked on in static horror, I let him down gently on his back, face pointed up into the achromatic autumn sunshine.

When I got a good look at him, I recoiled: his face looked ruddier than it had in life, though the skin of his hands and wrists had the slack cool-rubber feel of death. His eyes were still half-open, a slack grin still on his face.

Suddenly a shuddering Yvonne was at my side, her shoulder brushing mine as she put the tips of her fingers against the side of his throat. For long seconds we didn't move or speak, then she took her hand away and we looked at each other. "Hey, I know how to do artificial respiration," I told her excitedly, "he must be alive! We'll stimulate his breathing and get him going again . . ."

"No. No, Miller. He's gone . . ."

"Look at his color!"

"Miller . . . Miller, no. That's not it. The hemoglobin in blood, that makes it red? It bonded with the carbon monoxide instead of oxygen, that's why he looks like this . . ."

She closed his eyelids one at a time with a trembling forefinger. I reached out and gave her hand a stiff-upper-lip squeeze but she didn't seem aware of it.

I was going to try to say something comforting when I heard a car whispering down the Champs' curving drive. It appeared in seconds, a new gray Cadillac, driven by the silver-haired ever-natty Dr. Albert Cotter, whom I recalled telling several listeners once when he was in his cups at a smorgasbord that he *never* stopped to help at accidents, nor would he ever, because in Michigan there was no Good Samaritan law and he didn't fancy getting sued just for trying to save some poor son of a bitch's life—

Yvonne ran out in the road, waving her hands—Good Samaritan law or not, the good doctor could scarcely ignore this appeal. As Dr. Cotter got out and saw HG on his back, he pressed his right hand over his own heart as if he were ill, then turned quickly and went to his trunk, opened it, removed his black medical bag, and reluctantly approached the three of us.

HG on his back looked peaceful and composed, his complexion still rosy as a schoolchild's in midwinter, contrasting sharply with Dr. Cotter's seamed alcoholic countenance, now oyster-gray. The doctor's trembling lips pursed as he held the limp wrist and felt for a pulse that had no doubt been absent for some time. Finally he stood, swaying a bit, ignoring me as he turned to Yvonne. He took her arm and steadied her and they both took little mincing steps as though drunk over to his Cadillac. Dr. Cotter opened the passenger door, eased her in, then went around to the driver's side.

Neither looked my way as the Cadillac drove near-silently away, leaving me alone with HG.

I recalled HG speaking admiringly of Malcolm Lowry's "Death by Misadventure" and wondered if he'd imitated his hero's end. If so, I hoped the bond he felt with Lowry had given him some small comfort if not satisfaction at the end.

Ben

June 1944

Sonney's keeping a close eye on me and Ben to see how things are going to "shake down," as he says.

I been expecting him to do something about Ben, but he hasn't yet.

Ben's the main rooster in the barnyard, "cock of the walk and ruler of the roost" Sonney calls him.

He knows how much Ben scares me, but for some reason he hasn't done anything about him yet. Ben follows Sonney around like a dog, brushing up against his pantlegs. Ben'll go right along out to Sonney's berry patch where he grows blackcaps and red and black raspberries and'd go right into the patch if Sonney didn't shove him back with his foot or his cane, then pull the fencewire gate around to block him out.

Ben's almost half as big as I am—I'm five and small for my age. One of the few times I ever saw Sonney mad at my two-year-older brother was when Rex called me "Runt" about a week ago: "Don't you never, never, *never* call Miller that! It ain't manly, for one thing, and f'r 'nother you're two years older'n most of all he's your *brother*—and our main rule 'round here is, we all of us, *allus* stick together, just like the Allies . . ."

Sonney and Pearl never had kids and they set great store by taking care of me and Rex while our father is off in the South Pacific, "winning the war against the Japs," Sonney says.

When something happens, like Sonney catching Rex calling me Runt, cords stand out like wires in his brown neck.

Of course, by the time Sonney'd got near the end of ripping into Rex that time, most of the steam had gone out of him—"'Course I understand how you're a young'un and all . . ."

By then, Rex looked so sad from the word-trimming I thought he was going to cry. That made Sonney sad too, but just then Pearl came out on the stoop where the three of us were and asked if there was any around who'd fancy some peach ice cream, and if there was then they'd better have strong arms because it was going to require plenty of elbow grease and just maybe the youngest ones might get first claim on what was left on the paddles if they did their fair share of cranking.

✳ ✳ ✳

Our father, Turner Springstead, is in the Second Marines, where Rex and I hope he's killing lots of Japs—the more dead Japs the better, the sooner the war'll be over. Likely Turner'll come back to Ermine Falls and things'll change for us all over again. I don't remember much about our first, and I reckon only change, which was going from having our mother and father and being together to having our mother go off and leave us all alone. Then Turner went into the Marines and we came to stay with the MacReadys for what everyone calls "the duration." I can't even remember what Turner looks like by now.

I'm beginning to hope we can just stay on and on with Sonney and Pearl no matter what. I don't remember too much about our first life, except that none of it was as fun as things are with Sonney and Pearl. I don't want to take any more chances on changes unless I have to.

✳ ✳ ✳

Ben's big, mean, and a shiny black because Sonney puts flaxseed oil in his mash. His wings have red-gold colored tips and he has blood-red combs that jiggle when he tromps cocksure around the barnyard, always looking to keep the upper hand with his hens. He's always ready to go for any of the three younger roosters who're smart enough to keep their distance. Ben's from "fighting stock," Sonney tells us. He kind of struts in a steady bobbing march, looking this way and that, keeping an eye on things. What Sonney calls "his wartime duties."

Once, when I was headed out to the berry patch to the left of the barnyard to help Sonney pick blackcaps, Ben waited until I was just passing the big sliding doors to the barn and he charged me.

I lit out, running away from the barn toward the privy. When I got there I pushed the half-open door in and jumped inside and slammed the door and stood breathing hard in the sting-eye stink while Ben crowed and pecked at the door and beat at it with his wings.

When things quieted down, I stuck my head out and saw Sonney over to the west among his berry bushes, bent over, his blue bandanna out, mopping his eyes, laughing so hard he could hardly stand.

When he saw me watching him, he took to making believe he was just blowing his nose. *Honk*! he went. *Honk*!

To let him know how that made me feel, I didn't go over to the berry patch but went directly back in the house.

Pearl was in the kitchen drinking verbena tea and soaking her bad foot in hot water with mint leaves in it. I knew next she'd wrap it in a mullein poultice. "What is it, dear?" she asked. "Did that damnable rooster of Sonney's chase you again? Mark my words, that'un'll end up in my pot pies afore long. He's likely too stringy for roasting or frying . . ."

"Why's he Sonney's pet?"

"Oh . . . that man's always had a kind of special liking for things that are kind of out of round, if you know what I mean. Bothersome things. And people." She gave a long sigh. "Chickens and people, people and chickens," she said, but I didn't feel like asking her what she meant. "But I can tell you one thing, Miller, we ain't a-going to have much more of this business. I ain't a-going to permit it . . ."

* * *

That was two days ago and around 10:00 this morning after Sonney'd spent about half an hour with his hoe chopping weeds from around his berry bushes, he picked up his town cane and started off on the mile and a half into Ermine Falls for no reason Rex or I knew of.

I was a little miffed he didn't ask me along—sometimes it could be useful being the runt of the litter. Like that morning in April when Sonney came back with a red fox hanging over one shoulder from the crook of his everyday cane and carrying his 10 gauge shotgun on the other shoulder. After he'd put the shotgun away, it was me who walked into Guilder's General Store with him so everybody could see it.

Sonney walked along without his cane, hardly favoring his gimpy leg, the fox hanging down his back. He had the cane's crook caught in the fox's tied-together-with-twine mouth and held the long part in one hand and my hand in the other.

His big rough hand had never felt so good. The principal of the Ermine Falls School, Mrs. Gracious Carstairs, was in Guilder's when we came by and she went to her car and got her Kodak movie camera and came back and then had me and Sonney walk into town again, hand-in-hand with the fox hanging down his back just like we had the first time.

Rex was in kindergarten and, when he got home, Sonney was skinning out the fox and I told him all about it.

* * *

I don't know where Rex is right now, likely he's gone behind the barn, cut across some state land, come up on the old railroad grade and is taking that to town. Maybe he'll walk up the street to Guilder's and find Sonney and Sonney'll say, "Damn your hide, you're s'posed to be a' home," and then buy Rex a couple of licorice sticks and they'll both come home with Rex chewing the last of his licorice up in front of me (Yeah, but Sonney'll likely have got some for me too and maybe when he whips'em out I'll eat the whole two in front of Rex).

I look over my corn husker Sonney made me. It's a carved piece of ironwood, which Sonney claims is almost as hard as metal, about four inches long with a sharp point that passes through a piece of U-shaped harness leather that holds it to my middle finger—you slip the sharp end under the cornhusk to make a tear so's to get a good handful to pull off. "Now in your real cockfight," I'd heard Sonney telling Rex one day, "they strap steel spurs on over the ones on the cock's legs, makes'em real dangerous. One time I see a cock drive his spur right through the skull of the other'n's head. Generally they go for the breast, y'know, try to get that spur right in the ole breastbone—they's some can whang it in like when you see me drivin' a nail . . ."

I get my husker turned around so's the point's on the outside of my hand and now I got *me* a spur. Maybe I can do Ben just like another cock would. Sonney'll be proud if I do it all by myself. He's always urging me to not let Rex nor any other kids put nothing over on me, always telling me how I got to learn to be ready for anything, that I got to learn to rely on myself against a time when him or Rex or Pearl or Turner ain't around.

* * *

I put the husker in my overhaul pocket and in the barn I get the yard-long piece of gray lathing I'd found and been keeping. I figure to whack Big Ben with it and get him on the run and chase him down and knock him silly with the lathing and then drive the sharp point of my husker into his breast and if I can't get it there I'll pound it again and again into any old place I can. All the while I'll be ready to run for the outhouse, nip in and pull the door closed behind me if he starts to get the better of me.

I can do it pretty fast because I've practiced. I wiggle the lath like a sword, slash it through the air a couple of times. It goes *Whifffft*! *Whifffft*!

* * *

Sure enough, when I step back through the crack in the barn door there's Ben coming at me catty-cornered from the west in his kind of hop-run, his wingtips dipping and raising puffs of dust in a way'd look funny if I was up a tree.

Before he can get to me, I jump back in the barn and shut the door on him.

While he's still out there fussing I push the door back real quick, step out and swing my bit of lathing like a ball bat: *Whffi*!—*Whack*! Catch the sonofabitch right in the neck, he's over and onto his back, then up, his comb jiggling, skeltering toward me again, his wingtips raising dust, but I stand my ground and swing the lath again, hitting an upraised wing and knocking him sideways this time but not down.

As I lift my lathing again I see Sonney out of the corner of my eye Sonney rounding the northwest corner of the barn. He's coming my way, kind of hop-running himself, turning almost comically on the end of his everyday cane and his good leg.

I'll show Sonney what I'm made out of. As Ben stands and sees Sonney and tries to figure out what's going on, I run forward and kick him right in the chest, and he rolls over once and gets up and runs off toward Sonney, trailing one wing in the dirt like a dog with a hurt paw.

I drop the lathing, raise my hand with its ironwood spike sticking out like a dagger, but Ben, cluck-muttering, is almost over to Sonney and out of range.

Ben whisks behind Sonney, rubbing his head on Sonney's pant-leg like always, his one wing scraping the dirt.

Sonney drops his cane and bends down on his good knee, twisting to keep pressure off his gimpy leg.

He picks Ben up, tucks him under his left arm, and turns his back to me. But I can still see. Sonney's right hand, his strongest, covers Ben's head for an instant and makes a quick twisting motion as he pulls Ben's head off.

Ben's body fusses and kicks in Sonney's arm, but a lot less than I'd have expected.

Sonney tosses the head off to the left, where it falls onto the dusty ground Ben bossed, corn-yellow beak open and pointing up at the sky. A little blood dark as his comb dribbles onto the dirt.

Sonney flings the carcass in his other hand to the right, where it falls and flops a few times, but with no more spunk than you'd see from a hen after Sonney'd chopped its head off on a block of wood with a hatchet.

Ben's black feathers with the orangey tips shine like oil in the noontime sun.

* * *

Instead of the chicken and dumplings we were going to have that evening, we have pancakes and halved morels that Pearl dried out in the shop over the root cellar where long strings of them hang year-round. She'd put a batch into a pan of water to soak up, then rolled them in flour with salt and pepper and fried them in butter.

Rex can never get enough. Tonight he doesn't pay attention to anything else. I guess he doesn't know about Ben or that things are a little different for the rest of us.

("But you *tole* me to stick up for myself!" I almost feel like yelling at Sonney.)

There's a far-off look in Sonney's eyes, and he's quieter than usual.

Suddenly, not looking at any of us, he says, "Ben always was one for doing things all the way." His voice doesn't sound sad or mad. "Maybe that's why I kinda admired him. Don't think he really knew what he was up to, jumping you like he did, Miller. Who knows, maybe he seen you as competition for getting his head rubbed or for a handful or two of field corn every now and then. Maybe he thought you was after his lady friends . . ." His joke doesn't make Pearl smile.

Rex still isn't paying much mind to things 'cept those damned fried mushrooms. He's looking to get the last three or four in the gravy boat.

Sonney sighs. "Maybe he just got a little carried away . . ."

"Like some others I could name," Pearl mutters. I can tell she's mad because she clicks her teeth. I knew she'd wanted Ben to go, but now she doesn't exactly seem glad.

"Ever'thing'd be different if it wasn't wartime," Sonney says.

Pearl clicks her teeth.

"I don't expect he knew he was a danger to our tyke here. Anyhow he didn't suffer, so maybe he's luckier than the most of us . . ." Sonney still hasn't looked over at me.

"Oh for the Lord's sake, Sonney, it was just a *chicken*!" Snap! go Pearl's teeth.

"Yup. Well, reckon I'll maybe weed the blackcaps a little. Always kinda peaceful in a berry patch this time of day . . ."

I hold my breath, waiting for him to get up so I can ask to be excused and go after him.

Rex tears into the last fried mushroom and Pearl clicks her teeth again for no reason at all.

Sonney gets slowly up, using his cane. I wait until he's out of the house and then say, "Auntie Pearl, may I please be excused?"

"You may."

I get up and run out the door after Sonney. He's about halfway to the patch with a hoe over his shoulder when two of the other roosters, both kind of orangey with black wingtips and brick-colored combs, come running up and start fussing and pecking around in the dirt behind him. They follow him toward the berry patch like Ben used to do.

Chapter Twelve

I lay on my back, eyes closed, resting on the GI-taut spread on my bunk. Making it up thus in military fashion, as Rex had taught me, had seemed worth doing, though tomorrow or the next day Ardis Gray would come over and tear it apart: but for now a tiny point of order amidst the sloppiness and chaos of the day seemed a good thing.

Meanwhile, Rex was off calming and comforting Christy, who'd liked HG considerably and was terrifically upset. Rex'd taken with him the small pack of Kleenex he always kept available in his coupe's glove compartment for female tears.

It was already around 5:00, long after Rex and I had planned to be home; we might well be the last to leave, as near as I could tell, possibly beating out Sheldon Renfrew for the honor. As for Renfrew, he'd been flitting about the place in the aftermath of HG's death, going from summer folk to sheriff to friends of the family like a water-strider in a continuous cycle of condolences and soothing blandishments, his forehead like a carp's belly, his thin lips nearly bloodless. What had occurred was without precedent in the history of Les Champs du Roi.

The Skeegemog County Sheriff, Bud Watkins, and his Deputy, Jim Wagner, a hunting and fishing pal of Rex's, had spent a couple of hours patiently questioning those who hadn't already decamped (HG's demise seemed to have sped up several departures). Two state troopers from the Cadillac barracks, one a lieutenant, had turned up not long after Watkins had arrived, poked around for about an hour looking stern and extremely official in their blue and yellow cruiser, classy uniforms and crew cuts. Apparently satisfied with the way local law enforcement was handling things, they departed, leaving matters unequivocally in Watkins' sturdy farmer's hands.

Rex and I had always liked and admired Watkins, a man of legendary kindness and reliability. In his early forties, Watkins and Turner had been friends for almost twenty years, since the time Watkins as a deputy had jailed Turner for being drunk and disorderly shortly before Turner joined the Marines in 1940. Watkins had a kind of slap-happy look about him, mostly coming from his crooked grin, and a wonderful head of thick, wavy black hair. He'd been a Seabee in the war and, like Turner, had served in the South Pacific; and like Turner he'd been through Guadalcanal, though not Tarawa.

Of course, I was briefly interviewed, as were Rex, Duane and Ardis Gray. We all had pretty simple tales to tell: Yes, I told Watkins, at her request I'd gone out with Mrs. Goode to look for her husband . . . yes, he'd been drinking heavily and his wife feared for his safety . . . we came upon the running car in the garage, I shoved the door open and dragged Professor Goode—it seemed fitting I use HG's professional title—out into the air just as Doc Cotter came driving up . . . no, neither she nor I had any reason to think he'd be in the garage, we'd just happened on him—or heard the sound of his engine—more or less by chance. Yes, I told Watkins, HG appeared stone cold dead when I touched him, skin like ice (I didn't refer to his rosy color) . . . yeah, I'd seen him early in the morning around 7:00, and he looked somewhat drunk—no, I had no idea when he might have gone to the garage, no idea how long he might have been there, his Ford wagon idling away before we found him (for maybe up to three or even four hours, I privately guessed).

"Say hello to Turner for me," Watkins said pleasantly at the end of my ten-minute session, and shook my hand.

Watkins smiled his half-looped-looking smile and ambled off to chat with all-business Daphne LaBaugh Redpath down at the office in the lodge where she had taken in hand and was ministering to her decade-younger sister Yvonne. Earlier, Ardis told me, Doctor Cotter had given Yvonne a "calmative," and she was lying down "resting comfortably" in the apartment behind the office she and HG had briefly shared; soon, Ardis thought, Daphne would spirit her younger sister back to St. Louis. Yvonne had been "well enough" to speak briefly with Watkins and the State Police lieutenant, Ardis said.

At some point an ambulance from the Skeegemog Medical Center arrived to convey HG to the Schwartz Funeral Home in Skeegemog. Dr. Cotter had signed the death certificate, attributing HG's end not to "Death by Misadventure" as he would surely have liked, but to carbon monoxide poisoning.

Apparently nothing was deemed sufficiently out of sorts with HG's passing to warrant an autopsy. I heard "cremation" once on Renfrew's lips, twice on Ardis Gray's.

Someone had pulled HG's mocha—"shit brown," as Yvonne had called it in her earlier access of pique—Ford wagon around and parked it in the transients' parking area across from the lodge where it presently waited. For some reason it was sadder seeing it there than elsewhere, before the gloomy-looking and now horribly ironic sign: TRANSIENTS HERE.

Yvonne's turquoise and white "heavy Chevy" was parked next to it, but pointed in the opposite direction—toward the drive and the way out of Les Champs du Roi.

* * *

For something to do, I got up off the slippery bedspread and checked around in the cabin that was no longer a love nest for anything I might have forgotten. I was just about to go outside when I felt something through the sole of my tennis shoe. I bent down and found the arrowhead I'd given Yvonne last night in her "cubby." Perhaps she'd somehow dropped it in her distraction this morning when she'd come to see me and learned that HG had been by earlier: in any event, it would now never dangle between her breasts at the end of that gold chain as I'd envisioned.

I put it in the watch pocket—"rubber pocket," Rex naturally enough called it—of my Levi's next to the highly polished Petoskey stone Yvonne'd given me, then went outside.

I'd seldom seen the Champs so empty, so quiet, save when Rex and I came over in the winter after rabbits, when we'd drive in as close as we could get, usually to within a hundred yards of the entrance, then, shouldering our shotguns, we'd snowshoe in, Rex on his pickerels, me on eighty-year-old bear paws borrowed from Sonney MacReady. We'd hike around to the southeast corner where we'd get a good view of the snow-covered plain, the "champs," and beyond that the promontory with its cedar grove and secret cubby where Yvonne and I had made love as recently as last night (and certainly for the final time, I now realized), then the lake, a cool dark blue in winter, and the other side two miles across, where fields alternated with woods and where the winter sun reflected blindingly from the corrugated metal roofs of distant barns.

* * *

The exodus had really begun after Donnie and Jack Tudd had roared off in a combination of humiliation and dudgeon, even before the news of HG's death permeated the Champs, spreading a sense of horrible mystification like a virus; among others, the Gallaghers, Wahoolas and Steiners had left even as Sheldon Renfrew continued his circuits, darting here and there, wringing his hands, looking for someone to soothe, calm, comfort, console. Etta LaBaugh was likewise long gone, ferried off in one of the family's several Cadillacs just as the State Police had arrived; and by now Daphne and Yvonne were gone as well.

My last glimpse of Yvonne had been through the deeply tinted windows of Daphne's blueberry Cadillac idling next to HG's wagon and Yvonne's '57 Chevy. Around 2:30 I'd gone aimlessly down to the kitchen and wandered out and sat on the west end of the dining room porch which faced the lodge, arms around my knees, watching the Goodes' apartment through the porch rails.

Suddenly, there she was, clearly heavily sedated, walking haltingly as Daphne, arm around her sister's shoulders, guided her over to her blueberry Cadillac and opened the passenger's door.

Just before she lowered herself into the car seat, Yvonne looked blindly in my direction. I knew she couldn't see me and I felt an impulse to stand and show myself (and do-say what?), but I didn't move a muscle.

The angular Daphne slammed the car door decisively on Yvonne, got in the driver's seat, and backed out. Seeing Yvonne obscured through the deeply tinted windows was like seeing something dead on a lake bottom.

The Caddy disappeared.

So had it all really happened? Yvonne and I pulse-to-pulse in each other's arms, tasting, when we felt like it, the most intimate parts of the other as if it were the most natural thing imaginable? Sighing, groaning, sometimes crying out endearments? Had my lips really gone playfully back and forth from one to the other of her lovely nipples, teasing her in a kind of game requiring no instruction? And had they then started their inexorable journey downward?

Yes, yes, yes.

And had the anguished HG truly done himself in?

Yes, yes, yes.

* * *

During those moments after Yvonne and Dr. Cotter had left me and I'd been alone with HG, I'd sat down beside him, and looking away from him tried to speak. His face was still pointed up at the pale blue October sky and I couldn't bring myself to look at it: "Jesus, I'm sorry, HG, this is one of the pissier things I've seen occur . . ."

But it wasn't right and so I shut up. Then I got up, disgusted with myself, and turned to leave: "So long, HG," I'd said, "so long . . . don't take any wooden nickels . . ."

* * *

Rex was shaking my shoulder.

"Christamighty, Miller, wake up, it's a quarter of 6:00, how's about we get the fuck outta here? This shit's really starting to get on my nerves . . ."

"Uh . . . yeah. Okay. Suits me. G'head, I'll grab my stuff and be with you in a minute."

Outside with my knapsack over one shoulder, I rooted in my Levi's watch pocket, digging out both the black-gray-white arrowhead I'd given Yvonne and the highly polished Petoskey stone she'd given me. I shook them in my hand like dice, then flung them both back into the woods behind my cabin, an offering to who knew what.

In any case, I was sure the Petoskey stone Turner'd shaped and given me three years ago, battered from abrading against loose change in my pocket, was all I'd ever need.

I wondered what might have become of the manuscript of *Clumsy Partners* I'd seen on the passenger's side floormat of HG's Ford station wagon. Surely now, after all this, someone would step forward to become the work's advocate or, failing that, its custodian or conservator. Surely now that the author was dead by his own hand his manuscript would find some sort of life, if not the acclaim HG had yearned for. I recalled the composed look on HG's face in death, as if he'd grasped something the rest of us hadn't yet.

Meantime, Rex had ceased revving his engine and motioned through the window for me to hurry—he who'd taken his own sweet time tending to Christy. Still, this was a good time to have a brother and a father and a home to go to. So I gratefully scrambled into the '46 Ford's immaculate interior, chucked my knapsack on the floor, and leaned back against the resilient seat as my brother twisted the key, flipped the toggle and pressed the starter button.

I remembered suddenly that I'd left the bottle of champagne I'd lifted from the supply in the cooler under my bunk. So I told it what I'd told HG: "So long . . ."

* * *

"Too bad our good buddies Donnie Redpath and Jack Tudd missed the excitement," Rex said. "Probably would've done those two sonsofbitches some good to get a look at death close up, huh?"

"Sure as the fuck couldn't've hurt'em . . . so how'd things turn out with Christy?"

Oh, pretty good . . . we might not be too far from what they call being in love—'cept of course after Raina I'm kinda gun-shy. But Christy's kinda the same way for the same reason, she got burned once. Looks like the next step is, I gotta write her—she's got this idea how you tell more of yourself through written words than just through talk, or, well, affection, y'know . . . so I'm counting on you giving me a hand correcting my English and putting in a few high-class sweet nothings . . ."

I suddenly realized I didn't even have Yvonne's address, but realized, too, that it'd be a cinch to get it out of the Champs' office when we started putting shutters on all the cottages next week or so—if I wanted or needed it.

"She may have something there," I said, "who knows, maybe I'll test the idea out myself before I'm done . . ."

"Yeah? So what the fuck were you doing most of the time anyhow? You sneaking down the road and planking Silly Pillman or something? Christ, seemed like you was either working or sleeping or taking jumps in that ice-cold frigging lake . . . how many Trojans you got left? And thanks for soaking up my beach towel . . ."

"Got all of 'em . . . didn't figure you'd mind about the towel . . ."

"I didn't mind. Well, shit, if you wasn't going to make a run at Lindsay Noel, y'know, there was thirty-year-old Gloria Wahoola looked like she might have been in the mood . . . if you like 'em a bit older and on the plump side, that is, as I reckon I do—*used* to, anyhow . . ."

For a second or two I very badly wanted to tell Rex about Yvonne just as the father in Chekhov's "Misery" had felt compelled to talk to someone about the death of his son. But I couldn't, at least not now. Probably I should just keep my mouth shut and thank my lucky stars that I'd received such a lavish and compressed sexual education from such a luscious and knowledgeable female, and go my way—though the thought of never seeing Yvonne again left me feeling empty. I knew what Rex would advise: There's plenty more fish in the ocean, pal, just be ready to roll with the punches and cut your losses when things go bad . . . I heard HG's *Whah-hah-hah*! Echo somewhere in the back of my head.

We were well into the mile and a half downhill S-curve that ended at Silver River Bridge, and as usual Rex was taking it fast: he liked to do this last third of the S around 80 and see if he could get the sound he liked, a combination of the front wheels squeaking and the rear ones squealing a bit as they remained on the verge of breaking loose.

As soon as the Torch Rivera came into view on the left, we both noticed a disturbance on the right side of the road perhaps fifty feet before the Rivera. Rex applied his brakes gently and pulled over onto the right shoulder so we could regard the torn-up earth and shards of reflective glass and stray bits of chrome. It looked as if someone had fairly recently come around the corner pretty much like Rex—except unlike Rex, his wheels *had* broken loose and he'd rolled over right here.

"Jesus," Rex said, scanning the scene, "when it rains it pours, huh Miller?"

I thought of Yvonne, drugged and sealed in that tomblike blueberry Cadillac speeding back to St. Louis, and wondered if her tragedy- and drug-benumbed mind might not already be working on "our" story, now that its end had occurred and the day born for dalliance was concluded.

As Rex drove along Lake Drive and we looked out at Silverfish Lake on our left for the ten thousandth time, I tried to imagine what it might have looked like at night when Ojibway came in canoes and hoisted pitch flares in the night by whose light they speared whitefish. And perhaps had bows and arrows with arrowheads like the one I'd given to Yvonne, then returned to the woods.

When I shut my eyes and rested my head against the back of the seat I was shocked to see Lindsay Noel, feel her wraith-like hand pulling my head toward hers for a kiss, her blue and white checkered dress blousing forward so I could see her meager yet stimulating cleavage, her level gray eyes somber with love.

Where was she at this moment, what doing? Arriving in Ann Arbor, getting ready to do her homework for University High (which was no doubt a lot more rigorous than the Ermine Falls School)? Washing her hair? Squatting on the pot for a little tinkle? Maybe getting into bed, shuddering and recoiling as she worked her toes into cold spots in the sheets?

Billy Mink

October 1945

I felt I hated Turner when he decided to not let me go off to public school in September of 1945 even though I had turned six in June. It didn't matter to me that I was weak and feeling lousy from the mumps that I'd got in late July that even by late August had left me in kind of sad shape, "peak-ed," as Pearl says. And I was small for my age.

It wasn't so much his holding me back as that I thought he wasn't being straight with me when he explained it. I'd have another year to grow so I'd be getting an edge on the people in my class next year. And I'd likely have a few in my class, Turner'd said, who were even older than me. But I figured that what he'd really meant was that I was sickly and a runt and not ready for whatever was coming in school.

I watched him closely as he kept explaining, this big, strange, scarred-up man I wasn't sure I recognized when he got back from the war. Rex claimed he seemed the same in most respects, but I could tell he was surprised too. Turner'd got back three days after the second atomic bomb that'd caused Sonney MacReady to cry, with tears in his eyes, "Thank Christ! There's the final nail in the Japs' coffin! This'll bring our boys home, for sure!"

Anyhow, by mid-August my swollen jowls had shrunk so at least when I looked in the mirror I didn't always think of a cartoon mumps kid who needed a kerchief knotted on the top of his head to support his swollen lower face. But I suppose I still looked pretty damn peak-ed.

Rex was already in first grade and doing okay, and he was already a whiz at softball and baseball, what everyone called a natural. And since he was well and I was sick, that made everything a little worse.

"Another reason, pal, is 'cause this father stuff is pretty much new to me and I reckon I could use some company here myself, and y'know you really do look a little peak-ed, as Pearl likes to say. You need to get your strength up. You don't want to totter off when you begin your education—tell you what, Miller, if you're still dead set on it, I'll see if maybe you can't somehow start kindergarten half-way through, say after Christmas . . . what's your big hurry anyway"—now there was that kidding note I'd only lately begun to recognize—"where you got to be at a partiklar time and place for anyhow? Maybe if we take her slow and easy we can both help each other heal up a bit and'll both be the better for it, y'never can tell . . . why, what *is* it, pal?" We'd been sitting at the dining room table in our new-old house we'd been in just three weeks. Turner's usual muddy-looking cup of coffee, milk and sugar was at his elbow.

An awful look must have been on my face. Maybe even a tear.

So I blurted out my secret: "I want to learn to read."

A kind of light came into Turner's eyes and he turned toward me and away from his new Hallicrafter's Sky Buddy that sat on the dining room table that I could tell he'd been about to turn on: "I understand. And I wish I could help you, pal, but I only got an eighth grade edu—well, I ain't sure any'd call what I got an education. I can read Perry Masons and shoot-em-ups and newspapers just fine and anything I can't figure out right away I got a good dictionary for . . . I'm handy enough with math to run our business and to make out invoices and records and deal with the VA and do my taxes and things like that—but I sure as hell ain't a teacher. If I could afford you a tutor to come out and work with you I would. Hell, maybe I *can* find one, afford it or not . . ."

"You read just fine," I said, "you do it all the time so's you could sure as hell help me out—'sides I can already read some of Rex's Dick-Jane-Spot-Baby-Sally pretty good. I know the alphabet. I betcha me'n you could do it . . ."

Turner was silent for a while, looking east over my right shoulder at the cornfield you could see through the dining room window. Then he sighed deeply. "Okay," he said, "if you think so I guess we could take a crack at it on the proposition that something'll maybe be better than nothing. Maybe we could get you to where you might have a leg up on things for next year. Anyhow, it's hard to see how it could do either of us any harm . . ."

I put both hands under my jowls and tested them: "Don't worry, you was a soldier in the war. It'll work out, you'll see."

* * *

Earlier, Turner'd gotten four Green Forest books by Thornton Burgess from a guy he met at a car auction, and once he'd said that sometime he'd try reading them aloud to Rex and me.

I picked *Billy Mink* to begin with, and we got started there at the dining room table. *Billy Mink* looked awfully small in Turner's hands, or next to his big black dictionary.

First Turner'd read a sentence aloud to me: "Billy stopped and rubbed his nose thoughtfully. He was growing suspicious. 'I wonder,' thought Billy, 'if he is looking for me.'"

I'd listen carefully, and since I was good at it, I'd pretty much memorize the sentence. Turner'd read it a second time while I listened again. Then he'd hand me the book and I'd look at the words and more or less read it word-for-word back to him. I'd put my index finger on each word as I said it, staying with it until I got it right. Then Turner'd take the book back and ask me to spell a word aloud, coaching me a little when I needed it. After a time I got pretty handy at it except for words like "suspicious" and "thoughtfully."

After about an hour, Turner'd give me a list of important words from *Billy Mink* he'd printed on paper. I'd read them aloud. Then he'd take back the list and I'd sit there with a notebook and pencil and when he read the word aloud I'd pronounce it and try to write it down. Since I was left-handed, I had a hard time and kept getting my L's, R's, N's and D's the wrong way. Turner said not to worry, he could figure it out okay.

I knew it was working before Turner did.

Then one summer-warm day in early October I knew he knew we were making progress because he finished us up early, around 10:00, and said, "It's a real nice day, so let's close up the shop and take a little run on over to Thayer Lake and get in a couple of hours fishing. Maybe we can get us enough perch for a mess tonight, if not, what the hell, you'n me're entitled to a little fun. I don't know about you, pal, but for me this here's *work* . . ."

"You mean right now before we find out how Billy Mink makes out in 'What Bobby Coon and Billy Mink Did'?"

"Well . . . yeah. I expect I can prob'ly stand the suspense for a while longer. Tell you what, we'll take *Billy Mink* along and if things get dull on the lake we'll finish up that chapter. Maybe even go whole-hog and jump ahead to another in the book just for the fun of it . . ."

"Say, Pa, how come you say 'did-dunt' 'stead of 'didn't' when you read it aloud? . . ."

"Wellsir, maybe I ain't supposed to. Look here, see what you think—see here where he's made this what you call a contraction into two words? How he's got a space between d-i-d and n-apostrophe t? Wellsir, this book was printed in 1924—Jesus, that's only five years after I was born, so maybe they ain't doing things that way now. Maybe it's just straight out 'sposed to be 'didn't' with no pause . . . see, that's the problem, I just don't know a whole lot . . ."

"Well, let's us just keep on doing her like you was. I just wondered is all . . ."

"Seems likely I could be doing a whole lot of things wrong . . ."

"Nah, if you was I could tell . . ."

"Okay, if you say so, pal, that's good enough for me . . ."

I squinted up at him but he looked fine and pretty pleased with something.

It seemed to take him no time at all to get rods and tackle box together and scrawl a GONE FISHING sign to Scotch tape to the shop door.

* * *

So we got over to Thayer Lake around 11:00 in Turner's pickup and rented a rowboat and oars for a dollar from the Edwardses. I pushed the boat off and leaped off the mucky shore and into it. It seemed strange not to have Rex beside me, putting his shoulder to the bow along with me.

Turner rowed slowly over to the eastern shore that by now was all in the shade, and there we fished, saying little as we watched our red and white plastic bobbers floating amid the lily pads, waterbugs and dragonflies.

After near an hour without a bite, I began to daydream, thinking about how Billy Mink and Bobby Coon had dealt with the trapper and his awful traps. Then I thought of the times Rex and I had gone with Sonney on his trapline before Turner got back and of the emptiness I used to feel when Sonney pulled up a trap with a muskrat in it. Once he got a mink and I touched its wet fur and jerked my fingers back like it was hot metal because it felt alive while you could clearly see the thing had no more life in it than a drowned earthworm.

* * *

Turner could see I was day-dreaming. So he decided that we'd go ahead in *Billy Mink* even before we finished the chapter we were working on. And so he read aloud straight through the chapter where Billy Mink had "the wandering foot" and had gone out looking for something new and ended up at a farm, where he hid in a woodpile: "No one could get at him under that woodpile. He felt as safe there as ever he had felt anywhere in all this life. It made him chuckle to think how safe he was . . ." Turner seemed to like that part of the story as much as I did.

As he read on, I let go of any madness at him I had left in me, and I saw him for the first time as not just my father but as a person, apart from Rex and Sonney and Pearl, that I could rely on.

"From the henhouse, Billy went over to the big barn. This was another place just to his liking. Underneath it was dark, the very kind of place Billy liked. There were holes up through the floor. Billy sniffed at the first one he came to and he knew right away who had made that hole. It had been made by Robber the

Rat. Billy's eyes sparkled. It would be much more fun to hunt Robber the Rat and his relatives than to kill stupid, helpless hens."

Turner paused. "Well, that's the end of that chapter, pal. Just as well, it's getting on to one. We better get a wiggle on so's to get back before the bus does—I'd hate to have Rex to come home to an empty house . . . but I guess we got skunked again far's the fishing goes . . ."

"That's okay," I said, reeling in my line, reaching for the bobber as I hoisted it out of the water. I pulled the rest of my line in hand over hand, pulling off a chunk of pale waterlogged worm from the hook and dropping it in the lake. I pushed the hook into the rod's cork handle and tightened the line with the reel.

"The next chapter's 'Billy Has Good Hunting'—we can work on it after we do the one I just read and the one we were doing before," Turner said.

A fish jumped behind us and a bullfrog nearby went "*Galunk*."

"Hear that?" Turner asked. "That means for sure it's time to go home. This's probably our last day without a nip in the air."

"Suits me," I said.

Chapter Thirteen

"Busy day, huh, fellers," Turner said behind us. I was so glad to hear his voice I almost blushed. Though Turner was breathing heavily, neither Rex nor I had heard him come up, but neither of us turned around: we couldn't take our eyes from the twisted bright yellow wreck on our flatbed truck pulled up before the shop.

I recalled Rex's remark that it'd been a shame Donnie and Jack Rhymes-With-Pud Tudd had lit out before they got a chance to "get a look at death close up . . ." I especially remembered the permanent look on Jack Tudd's face which told you he was so accustomed to being disparaged he'd smile equally whether called prick or prince.

I was the first to turn to our father: "What happened? And how are they?"

Turner's green twill work pants and shirt were nearly black with sweat over his chest, armpits, belly and groin from his nightly exercise run. Just about every night, rain or shine, through three seasons and sometimes four, Turner jogged in his work clothes up the path behind our house to our let-go-wild apple orchard where we buried animals carrying two heavy dumbbells—I'd guess each at forty pounds—he'd made years ago from pieces of axle set into concrete poured into number 10 cans. Lifting and swinging the dumbbells vigorously, he'd take the thirty per cent grade up to the orchard, then cruise down its lee side on an overgrown logging road that ran into a dead end on the state-owned woods, then come back, covering maybe a mile and a half in his circuit. Back in the house, breathing heavily, he'd hurl his sodden clothing, including socks, underwear and bandanna into the washer, set it going and head for the bathroom in his blue terry-cloth robe, where he'd start the tub filling. He liked to sit in warm water nearly up to his neck for up to an hour or so, smoking a cigar and reading either *The Detroit Free Press* or the *Traverse City Record Eagle*.

Turner's breathing was beginning to slow. "Figured you'd likely know. No? Well, the two kids in it turned turtle there by the Torch Rivera, tossed the tall skinny drink of water who was driving out onto the grass. He hardly had a bruise on him, but the short fat one, he got tossed out too, but the car rolled over on him and killed the poor son-of-a-bitch instantly. Bud Watkins's had a busy day—he was coming down from the Champs and got there just after it happened. They got me out there about an hour and a half later. Bud was even able to get on his radio and reach the ambulance with the corpse of that guy who bought the farm at the resort, and so it ended up taking two stiffs at the same time over to Skeegemog. Like I say, the skinny one didn't have a scratch on him. There's a piece of luck for you, eh? Somebody said the two fellers'd been at the Champs' wedding . . . so I reckon you guys knew them?"

"Just pretty much at a distance," Rex said slowly, thinking.

Like me, he couldn't seem to stop staring at Donnie's squashed MG-TD: Donnie's "windscreen" with its gleaming chrome adjustable posts was gone, as was the "bonnet," as he'd taken pleasure in calling the hood, and the passenger compartment was caved in from where the car'd ended up on its top. There was no blood anywhere.

"Anyhow, neither of them was friends of ours," Rex said, carefully keeping contempt from his voice.

"Damn shame anyhow," Turner mused. "Hell of a pretty little car, too. I'll take it over to the confiscated lot at the Governmental Center in Skeegemog tomorrow morning early. That's a killer corner if you're comin' down the hill fast."

"Unless you know what you're doing," Rex said.

"*Especially* if you think you know what you're doing," Turner said, as if he'd guessed we knew more than we were letting on. "Well, hell, anyhow, good to have you back, guys. I'm gonna dump my stinking duds in the washer and take a bath . . . you guys hungry? There's chicken and lunch meat and stuff in the fridge . . . I had a cheese and tomato sandwich earlier, maybe'll have another a little later, we'll get back to our sort of routine tomorrow, if that suits you . . ."

"Suits me," Rex said.

"Suits me," I said.

Turner came a little closer, peering at us like a sergeant inspecting troops: "You look pretty bright-eyed," he said to me, "sort of like the cat they tell about that ate the canary—so you didn't join your fun-loving brother in polishing off all that champagne I imagine they had?"

"I kept pretty busy," I said. "Lotsa damned pots and pans and dishes. Christ, those guests'd foul one place with dishes, glasses, bottles and ashtrays, and when things got a little close they'd cruise off and find'em a new place . . . and I helped a woman I knew from before wax her car . . ."

Turner's eyes, light blue and directly on me, suggested he was musing on something other than my forthrightness: *The bastard's been up to something . . . now is it my fatherly duty to find out what? Or at this stage in the game do I just leave him to his secrets and try to not meddle?*

But before he could say anything further to me, Rex confessed: "Yeah, fact is that first night I got shit-faced and made a general fool out of myself. Didn't turn out so bad in the end, though, got me in with a real nice young woman there who goes to U of M . . . maybe later me'n her'll get together, you never know . . ."

"Well, you never ever know what's going to happen when your kids go off," Turner said, sighing. "Lucky for you guys fatherhood didn't seem so scary back when I was a young buck as it did when I developed half a brain much later on . . ."

He was joking, but nonetheless I could see something already receding in his eyes, as if he'd realized he'd obliquely touched on the subject of our mother.

"Might even write her a letter or two," Rex said.

"Well," Turner said, eyes coming back to rest speculatively on me. "I heard on the radio literacy's on the rise, and now I can see for myself it's true . . ."

* * *

As we watched Turner walk off toward the house, I wondered how much, if any, responsibility I bore for Harrison Goode's end, then answered myself: None, god-damnit, and I doubted any of it was Yvonne's fault—she could've been saintly and chaste as a mother superior at the Champs and the result would have been the same. *He liked the dead . . . grass was not green nor even grass to him; Nor was sun, sun, rose, rose, smoke, smoke, limb, limb . . .* Perhaps HG's end was assured from that moment Yvonne'd described when HG sat on their green sofa with the manuscript that had been returned by Fourth Class Mail "like a god-damned Sears and Roebuck catalogue" on his knees and a blank look on his face. Maybe the words "Fourth Class" had done the trick.

"Too bad it wasn't Donnie," Rex muttered, eyes on the caved-in cockpit and the sprung and twisted doors of Donnie Redpath's smashed toy.

"Well, anyhow, this'll give the survivor something to think about, eh? Likely make a good yarn to tell the brothers back at the frat house, hey . . ." I poked Rex in the ribs, he turned and for a few moments we wrestled half-heartedly, neither able to get any advantage on the other; but we tired of the horseplay quickly. "Shit, it's getting on toward 7:30, I expect," Rex said, glancing at the lowering sun. "Reckon I'll put my stuff away, maybe take a bath myself when Turner's done. Say, what the hell were you up to, jumping in the lake all the time at the Champs?"

"Dunno. Wild hair, I reckon." And couldn't help adding, perhaps to intensify the effect of owning a secret: "Hey, that's the tried and true formula for lackanookie, right?"

"You coming?"

"In a few minutes. Think I'll take me a little jog up to the orchard myself . . ."

"Jesus, swimming in freezing water, running up to the orchard . . . what's next?"

"Hey, you took your swimming suit too, you were the guy said how you needed hair on your ass for a swim this late—bet if Christy'd said to you"—I raised my voice and simpered, "'O Rex, my big strong guy you, how's about we take us a little midnight dip in the lake,'—well, I reckon you'd've done it."

"Expect I would. But you, all by yourself?"

"Yeah, well. It gave me a thrill." And there was a kind of thrill now in flirting with the truth to Rex; though burdensome, secrecy could add a certain kick to things.

"Hey, no school tomorrow," Rex reminded me. "It's Columbus Day . . . or the day after, actually, but it's a state holiday."

"Jesus! I'd forgotten all about it . . . so I guess tomorrow maybe you and me and Turner'll go to the cemetery, then . . ."

"Yeah . . . he takes that stuff seriously . . ."

Turner visited soldiers' graves once a year, though never on Decoration Day. And now I recalled that before we'd left for the wedding, he'd said we might go on the Monday off for Columbus Day this year—he liked being there when hardly anyone else was. He still had a hard time with gatherings or crowds of any kind.

"Hey, Miller, start thinkin' on love letters," Rex said as he moved off toward the house. "I want to get something in the mail day after tomorrow . . ."

"Yeah, okay—but I tell you what, you gotta take a crack at getting something down first, then I'll see if *I* can come up with something to spice it up a little . . ."

"You ain't going to do the whole thing yourself, then have me just look it over?"

"Nah . . . that's not how it works in the Springstead wordworks department."

Rex groaned and kept going toward the house.

I'd almost forgotten the existence of the Ermine Falls School, where Tuesday I'd be back to being a schoolboy shitkicker instead of a lover (could Yvonne have been right that once two people became lovers, they'd somehow always be such, no matter what?), doing my English, trig and journalism.

Since I'd finished most of my requirements, I had two consecutive study halls at the end of the day, where I'd often whiled away the time with Frank Yerby, Thomas B. Costain and Herman Wouk. And now Yvonne had told me I *must* read Flaubert, Fitzgerald, Faulkner, Welty, Wolfe, Dos Passos, Salinger,

Nabokov and a host of others: "I daresay you're going to find you're a lot closer to Fitzgerald's themes and preoccupations than you may ever have suspected, Miller . . ."

I picked up my pace as I headed for the path commencing behind the barn that went up into the orchard, thinking again, for no good reason, about Lindsay Noel and the time I'd seen her with her two friends, prancing in halter and shorts on her long tan legs beneath the gout of rain water, twisting her long hair like a rope to get the shampoo and water out.

* * *

As I jogged up the trail to the orchard, slipping and sliding in the same rocky ruts Turner would have negotiated earlier, I continued a fantasy begun when I'd watched Turner head toward his beloved evening bath: Turner was strong, kind, fearless, could be gentle and accommodating or steely depending on the situation, and it'd finally come to me what he really needed: Yvonne.

So I put them in the double bed in his room and turned them loose to fuck each other's socks off: Turner's skin was a little loose on him, no doubt from work and working out and squeezing most of the fat out of his system, but he was sturdy and muscular, well-hung, with a thicket of pubic hair with gray swatches in it. I wondered if he'd be reticent before a woman about the shrapnel scars on his back and legs and the bayonet scar on his left forearm. Probably not.

Yvonne reclined, spreading her legs, opening her arms to Turner as he, erected, breathing deeply, put one knee on the bedspread—yes, the one I'd had at the Champs with the ship's wheel designs and the texture of sex—and leaned forward, one hand on either side of her head, and as his mouth approached her open one, she inserted him into herself with one hand and looped the other around his neck and pulled him to her—

Shit. Something rankled, and I addressed my father silently: Lookie here, since there's no way of things *ever* happening with you and Yvonne, Turner, old hoss, whyn'tcha gitcher ass outta my head! I'm taking control over this here particular fantasy again, and she's *mine*, not yours.

I began thinking—even composing lines—of the witty letters I might send Yvonne, telling her how I wanted us to go on like Anna and Gurov, likened by Chekhov to "a pair of migratory birds, male and female, caught and kept in two different cages"; surely we could somehow manage to meet—"Rendezvous," Yvonne'd say—and kiss and hold and touch each other and make love again and again and again.

Panting, I reached the top of the hill and slowed, to walk in circles on the clearing, catching my breath.

To my left and straight ahead were state-owned woods, mostly hemlock, poplar, scrub oak and maple, but so glutted with brush and fallen limbs as to be nearly impenetrable.

The path straight ahead was the remnants of an old logging road and it continued for thirty yards, then turned north and turned into the steeply angled grade going down onto more state land, where Turner descended to his turn-around spot on his exercise run. There, close-together trees were latticed with skeins of viney bracken and fallen widow-makers formed obstacles for anything not built close to the ground.

To my right was our apple orchard whose trees still bore fruit though they'd not been tended or sprayed in years.

The sun had disappeared and the new moon, cloaked for close to a week now, had become a sharp, impossibly bright thin crescent that cast a beautifying light, making the haphazard angles of branches of the gnarled and twisted Jonathan tree toward which I walked seem made of tarnished silver.

A few small apples remained on some of the trees, while others lay scattered on the ground. I could see long grasses bent down into concavities under several of the trees where deer had bedded.

I looked up at that brilliant shard of moon now almost directly overhead, lifted my arms, fists clenching, to the heavens, and called out "*Yvonne*! *HG*!" My cries darted like whizzing embers into the night and were instantly absorbed.

But I'd scared a young doe asleep under a tree to my right, and she staggered drunkenly to her feet and stood quivering and half-asleep, spindly-looking as a foal, staring blindly at me as though I'd a jacklight on her: her nostrils flared, big mouse ears pricked; then, belying her frailty and tremulousness, she wheeled and bounded away in a series of graceful parabolic leaps, white flag waving, and disappeared down the dark side of the hill into deep woods.

My heart was pounding. I walked over to the spot from which she had risen and fell to my knees. The long grasses that had made her bed looked like woven silver in the moonlight and were faintly warm to my touch, and the instant I felt the fading heat I gave up Yvonne: No, I wouldn't write her, wouldn't make any move to see her again, ever, even if she returned to the Champs.

I rolled over on my back. The grasses were springy, comfortable, and for a moment I thought I could feel a last tinge of deer-warmth on my back.

I looked up through the gnarled limbs above me, and they appeared to be twisting, writhing clockwise, screwing themselves upwards into the night as if in urgent need of reaching that gleaming bit of moon.

Tomorrow Rex, Turner and I, dressed in khaki trousers and white shirts and maybe light windbreakers, would stand before graves of veterans Turner had known and some he hadn't, side-by-side, shoulder-to-shoulder.

Then, near the end of our visit, would come the part I dreaded, when we'd stand briefly before the three lots Turner had bought years ago for us. His spot already had his tombstone on it and on the plain granite stone was engraved:

TURNER SPRINGSTEAD
FATHER
1919-19

I'd hated that goddamn stone since he'd had it put there two years ago. Specifically, I hated the 19 awaiting its final two digits.

"*Why*, for Christ's sake?" I'd asked him again last year, almost angrily. "Why the hell don't you think you'll live into the new century? Christ, you'd only be eighty-one, hell, Sonney's almost that old now, and you're in better health than he ever thought of being . . ."

"Well, it just seemed a good idea at the time," he mused, the kindly look coming into his eyes as it often did when he understood his listener was in distress: "Tell you what, pal, if it keeps bothering you, I'll throw the son-of-a-bitch out, okay?"

"Okay," I'd said. "That a promise?"

"You can take it to the bank, son. This wasn't meant to disturb you guys, just to keep us in touch with how things work, maybe. It seemed a good enough idea at the time, but maybe it was a bad one . . ."

But it was still there! Well, tomorrow I'd call him on the promise he'd said was something you could take to the bank: Get rid of that goddamn stone! It offends me! And he'd do it. He never broke a promise.

I thought now of Thayer Lake, over by Clam Lake, about ten miles north of Ermine Falls, where Turner'd taken us numerous Sunday afternoons in those early years just after he got back from the war. Thayer was not much of a lake by most standards, which is maybe why our time there was so serene, as if time had slowed to a comfortable trudge just for us while the rest of the world was mostly elsewhere. The shoreline was rich and mucky and the prow of the rowboat we rented for one dollar for the whole afternoon cut a deep V. After we pushed Turner off, Rex and I could look back and see our sneaker prints coming to within a couple feet from the water's edge, when we'd jumped aboard. The black muck of the shore was so saturated the V and our footprints filled quickly with water.

Turner liked rowing. You could see the lines in his face relax as he took deep breaths and, with powerful but unhurried strokes, moved us toward our usual fishing spot.

Once established near the northeast shore, anchor overboard, tackle box open, hooks baited, there came a time when we did little but sit silently amid the lily pads and frogs and dragon flies and watch the water striders and water boatmen weaving around our red and white bobbers (beneath which I did not doubt hosts of sunfish, bluegills and perch swam idly about). As for ourselves, only our eyes moved for minutes at a time. Bites were few and far between, thus it was easy to drift into a lulled state induced by the alchemy of water lapping and occasional birds calling and waning sunlight still capable of faintly warming our limbs. Such doldrums required no speech or thought, only being there, and after a time you didn't give the slightest good goddamn if you ever caught a fish—if you ever had.

Sometimes, the afternoon dwindled until a particular moment arrived when the sun dropped below the horizon, leaving a refulgence of its wandering fire, then the last residual crimson would feather into dark turning afternoon into evening. And always at that moment, no matter that my father and brother were beside me and that there was nothing threatening in the offing, a grenade of sourceless fear would burst inside me, and not be dissipated until I heard Rex (he was in the middle, Turner at the stern, I in the bow) seat the oars in the oarlocks and begin to pull us toward home.

I got slowly up from my bed of sinuous grasses, grateful for the moonlight, surprised at my stiffness, and walked far enough toward the trail down to the house that I could see the moonlight spread across our house, cornfield, barn, and acres of pasture, now concealed from the road with stockade fencing, cluttered with the twisted car bodies and chassis that provided our living.

I lifted my eyes to the brilliant scrap of moon and tried to think again of Yvonne, but the only image that would come into my head was that of Lindsay Noel as she danced beneath a gushing eave trough, twisting her rain-soaked hair.

* * *

Turner was sitting at the dining room table in his robe and slippers when I came in, a large glass a few shades brighter than

HG's mocha station wagon before him—no doubt instant Sanka iced coffee with sugar and milk.

Turner's robe had huge bell sleeves and when he laced his fingers together the L-shaped scar on his forearm from a Jap bayonet in 1942 looked more livid than usual.

"You get anything to eat yet?"

"Not yet," I said. "How 'bout you?" I was by now so hungry it was a constant ache, yet I wasn't quite ready to ease it.

"Thought about it and discovered I wasn't hungry."

I wondered if the death wreck sitting out on the flatbed accounted for his lack of appetite, he who God knows had seen horrendous things in the South Pacific, especially on the Tarawa atoll called Betio.

The Sky Buddy was turned low and just before Turner turned it off, I heard, "President Eisenhower's decision to order the FBI to investigate the explosion which wrecked a Jewish Temple in Atlanta, Georgia, has upset—"

"You fellas around when the fellow to the resort checked out? Somebody said he was a college professor . . ."

"I went into the garage and pulled him out of the car and got him out into the open . . ."

Turner watched me attentively and waited.

"His wife was worried, he'd been drinking non-stop for weeks before he got there . . . to make it short, we found him in that old garage, you know, there to your right as you drive in to the Champs, where the gas pump's to your left?"

"Yeah?"

"Yeah. His station wagon might have been in there idling away for maybe three-four hours, though he was still kinda pink when we found him . . . from carbon monoxide bonding with the hemoglobin in his blood, Yvonne told me . . ."

"Yvonne?"

"His wife. Woman whose car I waxed last year . . . and this year. I knew her from before . . ."

"Any connection between him and the two young guys in the MG?"

"No . . . well, yeah. Yvonne was the skinny one's aunt . . . Rex tells me we're going to the cemetery tomorrow, that right?"

"If it suits you guys."

"Suits me."

"Yvonne, eh?"

"She's a LaBaugh—the old gal Etta's next-to-youngest daughter . . ."

"How young?"

"Oh, within spitting distance of thirty, I expect . . ."

The number must have been high enough for Turner to dismiss what I suspected he had begun to consider.

* * *

But now that I was off the hook, I could bear my secret in solitude no longer, and my skin grew warm with the need to share it with someone I trusted. And without any warning to either of us, I found myself spitting the bones of the story out to Turner in a non-stop burst, a technique he himself had occasionally put to good use: "Well, I don't know what you might suspect, Pa, but yes, we . . . I and this woman, we did have sexual relations—but her husband didn't figure into it, he was on a straight route to the cemetery no matter what, he was barely aware Yvonne was alive, which maybe had something to do with how we got together, but we knew each other for a couple of years and plain liked each other, and . . . well, I'd as soon not be a kiss'n tell kind of a guy, ya know, and far's the guy himself goes, gotta admit I kind of liked him and he seemed to take a shine to me too . . . he was a great talker, but he wanted an audience more than a helping hand, which I reckon he was beyond. But as for the woman, yes, well, hmmm, Yvonne, she was a wonderful woman, Pa, and we went into things with our eyes open, so to speak, and were honest with each other, nobody got hurt or screwed up and now I expect things to dwindle off into nothing, which is maybe just as well, oh, and say, along with everything else I got a list of a lot of writers I want to read before I go off to college . . . fact is I think I'll go read a little more Chekhov before I turn in . . . kinda hard to explain me'n Yvonne to anyone, but I . . . it . . . was okay, Pa . . . I think . . ."

Turner sighed, realizing he was going to have to either comment or remain silent. "Well, Miller, there's a lot of things I don't trust, but one I do is you and the second's my instincts—f'rinstance, I still think I was right holding you back from school till you were seven—"

"—Hey," I interrupted, "I never blamed you for keeping me back that year, it was a great year . . ."

"Same here," Turner said. "There'll never be another like it, and my trust in you comes from that year, son. 'Member how you followed doctor's orders and how I set you to walking and doing light dumbbell exercises? How we ate an ungodly amount of lunchmeat sandwiches and Campbell's tomato soup? How between the two of us you more or less learned to read with Thornton Burgess books before you was even in school? Remember *Billy Mink*? *Bobby Coon*? *Little Joe Otter*?"

"I remember it all . . . it was a hell of a year, Pa . . ."

"Well . . . listen, I think I understand enough of your situation that you don't need to give me the particulars, I've yet to be disappointed in either of you boys in any major way. And if I ever was, the fault'd be mine. Well, you know if you want or need my help or advice you know I'll give it to you guys without limit, you're my boys, my family, and I'll always give you the best I got, though in some instances that ain't going to be enough to do the trick. Whew. Maybe for now it's time for us to just say, 'Enough said'—what you think?"

"Nuff said."

"Put'er there, pal . . ."

I put out my hand and Turner took it: his hand was large, strong, callused, dry, the nails blunt and hornlike.

"You know," he said, "I think Rex may have a real case on that girl—I don't think he even knows or cares that the Yankees beat Milwaukee in the World Series six to two earlier today . . . unless in the middle of everything you guys was listening to the radio . . ."

"Don't believe either of us heard one all weekend."

"Hmmm. Must have been even better than I guessed. Well, since I've started my education a little later than you did, I guess I'd maybe better get on with it"—grinning, he lifted his Modern Library hardback of *God's Little Acre* from the table—"so see you in the morning, sleep tight and don't let the bedbugs bite . . ."

I burst out laughing. "Been a while since I heard that one," I said.

"May be a long time before you hear it again," Turner said, grinning, getting up, the Caldwell novel small in his hand.

He slapped me on the shoulder as he moved behind me, heading for his bedroom: "G'night, son."

"G'night," I answered, waiting until he'd reached his room and shut the door before I used a word I never had to his face: "G'night, Father . . ."

* * *

Donnie. Jack Tudd ("Rhymes with pud!"). Rex. Christy.

And Clover LaBaugh Budlong: what'd they think when they heard of the two deaths? When did they? Had they learned of both at once? Where had they been? What doing?

Instinctive prurience nudged me into imagining Clover and Jeff, tremulous with desire, heading for the depths of their king-sized bed when the phone rang in the Honeymoon Suite (In Traverse? Petoskey? Harbor Springs? Detroit? Ann Arbor?).

"HG . . ." I said, shutting my eyes, my voice barely a whisper. But instead I again saw Lindsay Noel in my mind's eye, twisting suds and rainwater from her long auburn hair.

That sickle-shaped scrap of new moon was high and bright now, so bright I half-expected it to evaporate in an incandescent puff like a handful of dried corn silk tossed into a campfire. Instead, it continued to belly gaily amid the stars, a gleaming wind-filled spinnaker.